BITTER POISON

BITTER POISON

A Village Mystery

Margaret Mayhew

This first world edition published 2016
in Great Britain and the USA by
SEVERN HOUSE PUBLISHERS LTD of
19 Cedar Road, Sutton, Surrey, England, SM2 5DA.
Trade paperback edition first published
in Great Britain and the USA 2016 by
SEVERN HOUSE PUBLISHERS LTD

British Library Cataloguing in Publication Data

Mayhew, Margaret, 1936- author.
  Bitter poison.
  1. Pantomime (Christmas entertainment)–Fiction.
  2. Murder–Investigation–Fiction. 3. Detective and
  mystery stories.
  I. Title
  823.9'14-dc23

ISBN-13: 978-0-7278-8580-7 (cased)
ISBN-13: 978-1-84751-688-6 (trade paper)
ISBN-13: 978-1-78010-744-8 (e-book)

All Severn House titles are printed on acid-free paper.

Severn House Publishers support the Forest Stewardship Council™ [FSC™],
the leading international forest certification organisation.
All our titles that are printed on FSC certified paper carry the FSC logo.

MIX
Paper from
responsible sources
FSC FSC® C013056
www.fsc.org

Typeset by Palimpsest Book Production Ltd.,
Falkirk, Stirlingshire, Scotland.
Printed and bound in Great Britain by
TJ International, Padstow, Cornwall.

For Lucy

'What is food to one, is to others bitter poison.'

Lucretius, Roman poet and philosopher

ONE

Major Cuthbertson was in his armchair beside the sitting-room gas fire, reading his newspaper and keeping a close eye on the clock on the mantelpiece. As soon as it chimed six silly pings he could get himself a drink without having to worry about Marjorie coming in and making a big fuss that he'd jumped the gun. She was busy banging pots and pans in the kitchen, trying out some new recipe she'd torn out of a magazine at the hairdresser's, but opening the cocktail cabinet early would still be a risky business. The old girl had ears like a bat.

The regiment had presented the cabinet on his retirement and it played 'Drink to Me Only With Thine Eyes' loudly whenever the lid was lifted. He wasn't sure if it had been meant as some kind of joke.

He turned another page and took another look at the clock. Either the big hand had stuck or the damned thing was going slow again. It had belonged to Marjorie's mother, which, in his view, was a pretty poor reason for keeping it. His late mother-in-law could still get at him, even from her grave.

He shook the newspaper hard. Things had come to a pretty pass when a man couldn't have a drink in his own house when he chose to. There was little else to brighten his days. Frog End was a nice enough village but it had to be said that it was a bit of a backwater. Not much of a life for a chap like himself who'd spent his army career in some of the world's hotspots. The highlight of the Frog End year was the summer fête, more than six months away, and now that Marjorie had vetoed him running the bottle stall he'd be reduced to being general dogs-body, heaving tables and chairs around for a pack of bossy women.

Still, thank God he'd managed to dump the job of treasurer on to the Colonel when he'd moved into Pond Cottage on the green. He hadn't seemed to mind. A pretty decent sort of chap, really. Played with a straight bat. He rather envied him, sometimes, for being a widower and having a free playing field, as it were. Not that there was much scope locally. He'd had his own chances, of course. Several women had definitely given him the green light. One of them – the lady of the Manor, no less – had unfortunately got herself bumped off just as things were hotting up. It had put the wind up him for quite a while in case the police had suspected him. Cramped his style no end.

In any case, he had to be careful. Marjorie not only had ears like a bat, she had eyes like a hawk.

He took another squint over the top of the newspaper. Dammit! Still seven minutes to go, according to that useless clock. Well, he was blowed if he was going to sit there and take it lying down any longer. He folded the paper, rose determinedly to his feet and headed towards the cocktail cabinet in the corner of the living room. He was halfway there when the door opened. He altered course smoothly, turning towards the window.

'It's not six o'clock yet, Roger.'

'I know that, dear. I'm just seeing to the curtain. I can feel a draught.'

His wife came into the room and sat down on the sofa. 'There's nothing wrong with the curtain and no draught, but there was something wrong with that recipe. I had to throw it all away. Luckily, I found a tin of corned beef. That'll have to do.'

He was used to having to make do with Marjorie's cooking. It had never been her strong point. In fact, she had seldom, if ever, had to cook until he had retired, or to clean either. On postings abroad there had always been servants to do all the work. Now there were none.

No chance now of a decent stiffener or two in peace.

'Not to worry.'

'I'm not worried, Roger, just annoyed. Magazines should test recipes properly before they inflict them on their readers.'

'I quite agree with you. No consideration these days. No standards. Country's going to the dogs.'

He glanced towards the mantelpiece while Marjorie pounded a cushion, settling herself in. Still five minutes to go.

'By the way, we finally reached a decision at the meeting today. And not a moment too soon. Far too much time has been wasted arguing.'

He had no idea which meeting she was referring to. Some committee, he supposed. She was usually chairman. Or chairperson. Or whatever they called it now.

'What about?'

'About our Christmas show, of course. The Frog End Players do one every year, Roger, in case you've forgotten.'

He had vague memories of last year's performance at the village hall. *Puss in Boots*, or was it *Cinderella*? Whichever it was, the principal boy had been played by some callow youth. Principal boys should always be girls, and have very good legs. It was tradition and all that. At least old Toby Jugge had provided a bit of light relief as the Dame. Of course, Marjorie hadn't understood any of his jokes. A bit near the knuckle, some of them, it was true, but that was the whole point. Keep the adults amused as well as the kids. Only fair. And that bedtime striptease Toby had done had brought the house down.

'What did you decide?'

'We're going for *The Snow Queen*.'

'The what?'

'The Hans Christian Andersen story, Roger. Rather an inspired choice, I thought. Quite different from the usual pantomime. We're going to re-tell it in a very simple form for the village children. It's a charming story of good triumphing over evil. We'll be doing three performances.'

'Never heard of it.'

'That doesn't surprise me.'

'Well, I hope the principal boy's going to be a girl this time.'

'I'm sorry to disappoint you, Roger, but there's no principal boy.'

'No principal boy?'

'That's what I just said.'

No long legs in fishnet tights and high leather boots. No

striding up and down. No slapping the thigh. What was he supposed to look at?

'What about a Dame?'

'Certainly no Dame.'

No outrageous frocks. No striptease. No blue jokes. Nothing to laugh at at all.

'Will Toby get a part?'

'There will be nothing suitable for Mr Jugge – I'm glad to say.'

It was going to be even worse than he'd thought.

'What's it about, then?'

'A wicked Snow Queen with a heart of ice steals a boy called Kai and carries him off to live in her palace at the North Pole.'

'Damned odd name for a boy.'

'He's foreign, of course. Danish, I imagine. A glass splinter from an evil sorcerer's broken mirror has pierced his eye and another his heart, making him see ugliness in everything and behave cruelly to everyone. When the Snow Queen kisses him the splinters turn to ice and he falls under her spell.'

'Bad show.'

'But Kai's best friend, a girl named Gerda, sets out on a long and perilous journey to save him, even though he's treated her badly.'

The Major rustled his newspaper. 'Doesn't sound much fun.'

'It's not meant to be fun, Roger. It's a fairy tale, not some vulgar pantomime. And there are lots of other jolly good parts: a kindly old grandmother, a witch with an enchanted garden, a prince and princess, two wise women, a band of robbers, a raven and a reindeer, hobgoblins, talking flowers, dancing snowflakes, guardian angels . . . plenty of roles for extras, you see. Gerda encounters them all on her brave quest to find and rescue Kai.'

The Major wondered if he could get away with a convenient bout of flu, carefully timed to stretch over the three performances, but doubted it. Marjorie was never sympathetic to illness, even if it was real.

'Happy ending, I hope?'

'Of course. Gerda battles her way through blizzards to the

Snow Queen's palace and finds Kai at last. Her hot tears melt the icy slivers in his eye and heart. He is freed from the Snow Queen's spell and becomes his true kind self again.'

'Thank God for that!'

'Now that Patrick is no longer with us, I'm to take on the job of director. Everyone insisted.'

Patrick, he remembered, was the long-haired actor fellow who had bit-parts in TV soaps. He'd been directing the Frog End Players for years, throwing his weight around as though he were Laurence Olivier. 'What happened to him?'

'He moved to London.'

'Good thing too, if you ask me.'

'I don't, Roger, but as it happens, I agree with you. It's time for a fresh approach and I think I can provide that.'

The Major's mind went back to the amateur dramatics they'd taken part in at various army postings abroad. The image of Marjorie in the Lagos production of *Charley's Aunt*, playing Donna Lucia D'Alvarez, the aunt from Brazil where the nuts come from, was still seared on his brain after more than twenty years.

'Well, I'm sure you'll do a very good job, dear.'

'I wondered if you might like to be one of the robbers, Roger, but then I decided you'd be much happier behind the scenes.'

Shifting them around, presumably. Like last year.

'So, who's going to be the wicked Snow Queen?'

'That has yet to be decided.'

'How about Mrs Pudsey? She'd frighten everyone all right.' Mrs Pudsey, he remembered, had once been a disastrous Fairy Godmother – hissed and booed by mistake.

'Mrs Pudsey will be offered a different role. The Snow Queen is intended to be very beautiful as well as evil.'

In that case, they're going to have a real problem casting her, he thought to himself. Very beautiful females were thin on the ground in Frog End, as he well knew.

'Well, what about that woman who's just moved into Hassels with her husband?'

'I haven't met her.'

Nor had the Major, but he had seen her briefly from a

distance as he had driven by the house. She had been coming out of the front door and he'd slowed the Escort enough to be able to mark her down as rather promising. Not in the first flush perhaps, but definitely a looker. Glamorous was the word. London clothes, if he was not mistaken. London hair, too. You could always tell. Well above the average for Frog End. 'Her husband's in television, so they say.'

'So who says?'

'Some chap at the pub. He makes some sort of travel programmes, apparently.'

'That doesn't mean that his wife knows anything about acting, Roger.'

He shrugged. 'Just a suggestion.'

At long last, his late mother-in-law's clock started its chimes. Like an obedient old dog still commanded to 'stay', Major Cuthbertson waited until the sixth one had died away before he stood up.

'Sun's over the yardarm. What'll you have, dear?'

'A very small sherry, Roger.'

'Drink to Me Only With Thine Eyes' began as he opened the lid. If only he could find out how to disconnect the bloody thing. He measured Marjorie's syrupy Bristol Cream into a glass and handed it to her. The trick now was to position himself so that her view of the cabinet was blocked and he could pour himself a hefty slug of Teachers, plus the merest drop of soda for a fizzy effect. He returned to his armchair with a jaunty step and raised his glass with a flourish.

'To the Snow Queen. And all who sail with her.'

TWO

The grandfather clock in the Colonel's sitting room at Pond Cottage had finished striking the hour and he stoked up the log fire in readiness for his neighbour's arrival.

Naomi Grimshaw was seldom late for things and almost never late for their customary evening drink. On the day that he had moved into the cottage a year and a half ago she had called on him and accepted his polite invitation to join him in a glass of Chivas Regal with alacrity. The habit had continued. As she had told him frankly on that first occasion, she could rarely afford to buy a decent brand of whisky and he had sometimes wondered whether it was the Chivas rather than himself that had motivated her.

Whatever it had been, she had proved to be a wonderful neighbour. Widowed, like himself, and about the same age, she was helpful, no-nonsense and full of practical advice on cooking, gardening and coping with domestic affairs of which he knew nothing. Under her expert guidance, the Pond Cottage jungle had been cleared and the long-lost pond rediscovered and dredged, and with the aid of her simple recipes he had learned to cook basic dishes. She had also taught him how to work a washing machine and a vacuum cleaner, neither of which he had ever touched before. In addition, she was an entertaining purveyor of tittle-tattle and gossip. Frog End, reduced to a single pub and no shop, might appear to be the sort of boring place where nothing much happened but, as he had discovered, this was far from the case. Beneath the placid surface swirled a positive maelstrom of intrigue, scandal and misbehaviour, with a surveillance network to rival the Russian KGB in its ruthless efficiency, not to mention the fact that two murders had taken place in the village since his arrival. In both cases, he had unwittingly become involved in the investigations leading to the identities of the murderers.

He gave the fire another prod with the poker so that the
flames flared up brightly and crackled. There was something
immensely satisfying and companionable about a real wood
fire. No substitute would do, in his opinion. It was well worth
all the log-carrying and sweeping out to have it there in the
cold, dark evenings, blazing away cheerily in the inglenook that
had been discovered behind a hideous tiled fireplace when the
cottage was being renovated.

Thursday, the torn-eared, black and tan stray moggy, named
after the day of the week when he had first turned up, evidently
agreed with him. He was, as usual, in his favourite winter
place, curled up at the fire end of the sofa, and there he would
stay until it suited him to go into the kitchen and sit in front
of his bowl, waiting for a gourmet dinner to be served. The
bowl was marked DOG but fortunately Thursday, for all his
native savvy, was unable to read.

As the Colonel went to sit down in his wing-back chair,
the old cat opened one eye, stretched out a paw to claw at the
sofa cushion and then went back to untroubled sleep again.
His days of worrying about where the next meal was coming
from were over since he had decided to make Pond Cottage
his permanent home.

The grandfather clock had struck half past six before Naomi
finally hammered at the front door. It was raining hard and
she was wearing a waxed cotton coat reaching to her ankles
and fitted with a long front zip and a number of flaps and
pockets secured by leather straps and brass buckles. It came,
he knew, from Australia, and had been brought over as a
present for her by her daughter-in-law on a visit to England
last year. Apparently it was intended for riding a horse in the
Outback during the Wet. Helping Naomi out of it, once in,
was a complicated business, but they accomplished it successfully from past experience. Underneath, she was wearing one
of her tracksuits – this one in an eye-watering shade of neon
pink – with her white moon-boot trainers on her feet. Her
thatch of short grey hair was beaded with raindrops and when
she shook her head they flew about the hall.

'Sorry I'm late, Hugh. The bloody pantomime meeting
dragged on forever, all arguing about what it should be this

year. In the end they had to agree on something – we're two weeks late starting rehearsals as it is. Then I had to feed the dogs when I got home. I'd just finished doing that when the phone went. Some woman I knew a hundred years ago, phoning for a chat. Couldn't get rid of her.'

He hung the Outback coat on the hall stand. 'The usual?'

She rubbed her hands together. 'Rather!'

He led her into the sitting room, which, naturally, she could have found blindfolded. She scooped up Thursday and deposited him at the other end of the sofa, taking his place close to the log fire. It was a scene that the Colonel had witnessed many times before. In order to save face, the old cat feigned sleep, legs dangling, but the slits of his eyes glinted and gleamed among the black and tan fur. Naomi was not a cat person, as Thursday was well aware. She had two Jack Russell terriers to prove it – not that they had ever been unwise enough to test the sharpness of his claws.

The Colonel poured three fingers of whisky into Naomi's glass and added a splash of water. No ice, which she considered a waste of space. His own measure was the same but without the water. He sat down in his chair and raised his glass to her.

'Good health, Naomi.'

She lifted hers, gripped firmly in her large, square hand. 'Same to you, Hugh.'

'So, what's this year's pantomime to be?'

'It's not a proper panto at all. They've decided to adapt *The Snow Queen*. The Hans Christian Andersen fairy tale.'

'I can't say that I know it.'

'It's about a wicked Snow Queen with a heart of ice. Some evil sorcerer has created a magic mirror that reflects everything as ugly and mean. The mirror breaks into trillions of splinters which fly around the world and one of them gets into a little boy's eye and another into his heart so that he sees things as they are in the mirror. When the Snow Queen happens to come by on her sleigh, the boy falls under her spell and she takes him off to her ice palace in the frozen north. In the end, he gets rescued against all the odds by his brave and faithful girlfriend who's helped by a raven, a reindeer and two weird old women. I've left quite a bit out but I think that's the general idea.'

'Not very merry for Christmas.'

'The idea is that they'll simplify it for the younger kids. Lionel Peters is writing a script.'

'Lionel Peters?'

'You know. Our tame Local Author. He does articles for the village mag and he once had a book published. I've no idea what it was about. Marjorie Cuthbertson's going to direct now Patrick's gone off to London. I warn you, she'll be on the warpath for people to muck in – extras, scene shifters, working the spotlights . . . all that sort of thing.'

'Mrs Bentley has already tried, and failed, to persuade me to join the Players.'

'Yes, so you told me. But as I told you, Hugh, Flora Bentley and Marjorie Cuthbertson are two very different people. Besides, you don't have to join officially. You'd just be lending a helping hand. Doing your bit.'

'Will you have a part?'

'Lord, no. I'm hopeless at acting. I just make myself generally useful. Last year I was prompter. Jolly hard work. Everyone always forgets their lines. But it's all rather good fun. Community spirit and all that. We're lucky the village hall has a proper stage and curtains and that room off the back for a dressing room.'

He was familiar with the cramped stage and the jerky progress to and fro of the faded red velvet curtains, not to mention the dangerously rickety steps leading up from the hall.

'What about costumes?'

'We hire them from a company for the principals. Otherwise, people make their own or scavenge around. *The Snow Queen* will need something extra special, I suppose – lots of silver and glitter. Thora Jay's going to do the principals' make-up again, so we don't need to worry about that.'

The name was unfamiliar to him. 'Have I met her?'

'If you have, you've probably forgotten. She used to work as a professional make-up artist and now she's an OAP in Frog End, like us. Widowed, too. She can make almost anyone look good. The odd thing is she never wears any make-up herself. Fades into the background. You really wouldn't notice her.'

Nobody could not notice Naomi, the Colonel thought, smiling to himself. Eccentric clothes, baying laugh, larger than life. You could neither miss her, nor forget her.

'How do you manage the scenery?'

'It's all made and painted in the village. It's surprising how talented some people are. You didn't see *Puss in Boots* last year, did you?'

'My daughter, Alison, was staying.'

'That's no excuse. You'll have to come this year.'

'I'm looking forward to it.'

'Don't lie, Hugh. You'll try to get out of it again, but if Marjorie Cuthbertson has anything to do with it you'll find yourself roped in somehow.'

'Couldn't I just be in the audience?'

'I wouldn't count on it. I'd go for scene-shifting if I were you, unless you want to find yourself playing a dastardly robber.'

'I'll remember that advice.' He went to put another log on the fire. 'I take it your son and his family won't be over from Australia this Christmas?'

'No, thank God! It was a nightmare last year. The cottage is too small and the kids are too noisy. And my daughter-in-law never stops complaining about our weather. They're going to come next summer and go off and look at castles and all the old things we've got that the Aussies haven't. That'll keep 'em busy.'

'Let me know if I can help. Maybe I could organize a trip to Bovington Tank Museum?'

'Good idea. You took your grandson there, didn't you?'

The trip to the museum with Eric had been a big success.

His five-year-old grandson had come to stay at Pond Cottage when his daughter-in-law, Susan, had gone into hospital with a threatened miscarriage. The Colonel had found the boy very spoiled and difficult to warm to, until they had gone together to see the tanks. They had toured the Challengers and the Shermans, the Matildas and the Panzers and the Crusaders, and the Colonel had given a full account of each: number of

crew, armaments, capacity and all the interesting – and sometimes gory – details. They had sat in a replica World War
One trench and a World War Two shelter, had both had a go
at the rifle range and blown away German tanks with the PIAT
gun. The visit had ended with lunch at the museum restaurant
where Eric had eaten fish and chips with big dollops of tomato
ketchup, drunk two sugary Fantas and finished with a double
chocolate ice cream – all things strictly forbidden by Susan.
A male bond of shared secrecy had been forged between them.

He said, 'My daughter-in-law wants me to spend Christmas
with them in Norfolk.'

'Oh dear! Are you going?'

'I ought to. I've only visited once since they moved there.'

He had prevaricated inexcusably when Susan had phoned
to issue the Christmas invitation but memories of his previous
visit were still strong. The bleakly lit house, the depressing
furnishings, the relentlessly nutritious diet, the lack of whisky,
or even wine, the absence of a real log fire . . . and at Christmas.

'Eric and Edith will be ever so upset if you don't come,
Father,' Susan had said.

It was always Father, never Hugh as he would have much
preferred to be called. Eric might be a bit disappointed by his
absence, perhaps, but he doubted that his six-month-old granddaughter would mind at all.

'As a matter of fact, Susan, I was wondering if you might
be able to come here?'

'Oh, I don't think we could do that, Father. I'd have to bring
the turkey and all the trimmings in the car with us.' She'd
sounded shocked at the idea.

'No need for that. I can cook quite reasonably now. I could
do everything here.'

'Eric can't eat lots of things – he's quite allergic, you know,
and we have to be very careful. He had to go to be tested at
the hospital after he got a bad reaction to nuts. His throat
swelled up and he couldn't breathe properly. It was awful. We
can't ever have shop Christmas pudding or mince pies. They
might both have nuts in.'

'I'm very sorry to hear that. We'll have something else,
then. Whatever is safe.'

'I'm afraid it wouldn't do at all, Father. Eric's used to our Christmases. I always do everything just as he likes. It's very important with children, you know.'

He did know, having been one himself, long go, and had two of his own. It was true that family customs and traditions meant a lot.

'I could take him to the Tank Museum again. He liked that.'

'Christmas is supposed to be about Peace on Earth, not War and Weapons.'

She had wound up the unsatisfactory conversation by telling him about yet another desirable bungalow that had come up for sale nearby.

'It's a very good price, Father. Quite a bargain and it would suit you perfectly. Easy to look after and just a very small garden that would be no trouble. You could view it when you come for Christmas.'

Her determination to have him living down the road so that he could be kept under even closer surveillance than with the Frog End KGB was undiminished. He had once spoken frankly on the subject, risking offence, but all to no avail.

He said to Naomi now, 'I asked them to come here instead, but I don't think that's going to work.'

'Tricky things, families. Especially at Christmas.'

He had no need, at least, to worry about Alison. She had been invited to go skiing in Zermatt with friends. Much as he would have enjoyed her company at the cottage, it would be a great deal more fun for her in Switzerland.

'What will you do, Naomi?'

'The same as I usually do. Spend it on my own with the dogs. It doesn't worry me. It's just another day.'

That was where Naomi had the advantage of him, he thought. Christmases past and present or those still to come meant nothing particular to her, whereas he had found them unbearably sad since Laura's death twelve years ago. The carols, the cards and the tree all conspired against him. There was no escape from bittersweet memories. Or from the loneliness.

'I think I'll have to go quietly.'

'Well, you'll still be here for *The Snow Queen*. They're doing three performances during the week before Christmas.'

There would be no getting out of it, he realized. He changed the subject adroitly on to one close to Naomi's heart.

'Those hellebores Ruth gave me last year are starting to flower already. I noticed them this morning.'

The daughter of Lady Swynford of Frog End Manor who had been murdered at the summer fête last year, Ruth had inherited the big house on her mother's death and, rather than selling it to developers, she had started a business growing plants for sale at the Manor. Naomi had already given two gardening talks there which had been a great success and other speakers were being roped in as well. When Ruth had finally had the sense to marry the local GP, Tom Harvey – a thoroughly good man if ever there was one – the Colonel had been extremely touched to have been asked to give Ruth away at the wedding, standing in for her late father.

He had planted the hellebores outside the kitchen where he could observe them from the window. The white buds he had just spotted would unfurl themselves slowly and bashfully and he would have to lift their heads in order to admire the delicate purple colour and greenish-yellow centre inside.

Naomi said, 'Cut off any old leaves in the spring, now they're established. It shows off the flowers better and it will help ward off any leaf spot. And give them a top dressing of general fertilizer. I'd plant some more if I were you, Hugh. Hellebores are excellent creatures and very easy. They tend to prefer semi-shade and damp soil and some shelter from cold winds; other than that they're not fussy. I've got some December Dawn I can let you have in the early spring. It's rather a nice soft pink.'

Not only had she been generous with her time and advice on transforming his jungle but also in donating all kinds of seeds and cuttings and clumps from her own enviably beautiful garden.

'That's very kind of you, Naomi.'

'Not really. I could use the space. Those Three Ships I gave you will be flowering before Christmas with any luck.'

She had given him an expertly divided clump of snowdrops – 'in the green' as she'd told him, using gardeners' speak.

'Much better than those dry, dusty old bulbs people buy.' He had been guilty of doing exactly that from a catalogue the previous year, choosing snowdrops with nice names and nice looks in the pictures: Merlin, Wendy's Gold, Magnet, Ophelia and Augustus, as well as the common wild kind. He had planted Naomi's Three Ships in a place of honour round the lilac tree. She hadn't laboured the point, but he had discovered later that it was a rather rare creature and of particular beauty. Whatever their names or pedigree, snowdrops were something to look forward to – the earliest and bravest of the brave spring bulbs, defying the winter gloom. The aconites would be waiting in the wings, together with the crocuses – soon to be followed by the daffodils that he had planted randomly in the long grass at the far end of the garden, attempting to ape Naomi's casual style.

'I'll take a look tomorrow and see if there's any sign of them yet.'

'I'll be able to let you have some of my winter irises, if you like, after they've finished.'

He had secretly coveted the small, lilac-coloured flowers growing serenely along Naomi's garden wall. 'Won't they mind?'

'Not if I just put a spade through one end. No need to disturb the rest. If I fill in the hole, they won't even notice. Find it a nice, sheltered spot, chuck 'em a bit of water and a feed and then nothing. They'll thrive on neglect and go on flowering for years. Did you decide what to do about the delphiniums?'

'Give them a chance, like you said.'

'Good thinking. They might surprise you. Did I tell you that Ruth has asked me to give another talk at the Manor in February?'

'No, you didn't.' He'd missed her last one because she had forgotten to mention it. 'I'd like to come. What's the subject?'

'A Practical Introduction to Seed-Sowing. It lasts for two hours and I'm supposed to give a demo of how to sow, prick out seedlings and pot on young plants. Four pounds a ticket. Not sure people will want to pay that much.'

'I'm very sure that they will.' Naomi's previous two talks

had been sell-outs, not surprisingly. She knew what she was saying and she said it well. Everyone could hear every word.

'Hope you're right.' She took a swig from her glass. 'Of course, you could start some seeds off in that shed of yours as soon as the weather warms up, Hugh. If you took down the sacking over the windows they'd get enough light.'

He had no intention of doing any such thing. The sacking was there precisely so that Naomi couldn't peer in, or anyone else for that matter. The shed was his private retreat. A bolthole from the world. A sacred sanctuary. A refuge from the likes of Mrs Bentley, doyenne of the summer fête cake stall, who had called at Pond Cottage with the express, though failed, purpose of recruiting him to the Frog End Players. It also provided a place where the lawn mower, garden equipment and a variety of other useful tools and implements could be kept in tidy order, as well as a large quantity of nails, screws, nuts and bolts which he had sorted into glass jars, ranged satisfyingly along a shelf. And he had bought himself a proper workbench with a useful compartment and a vice at one end. It was not, and never would be, a greenhouse.

He said firmly, 'There wouldn't be room.'

'Are you still doing those models, then?'

'Not at the moment.'

He had made several of them from shop-bought kits, beginning with a World War Two Matilda tank which Naomi had managed to glimpse through the window in progress on his workbench. He had since moved on to a Type V11 German U-Boat, a Royal Navy battleship, a Lancaster bomber and a Hurricane fighter. The Lancaster and the Hurricane were suspended on a fishing line from the shed roof – the bomber climbing, the fighter diving.

After the tank incident, he had successfully prevented Naomi from seeing inside the shed at all by means of the sacking curtains and by locking the door. Lately, though, he had spent very little time in there himself. The days were too cold and too dark. He had plans to run an electricity cable out for lighting and to buy some form of heater – plans that would be kept to himself, like the plans he had to try his hand at some proper woodworking. Naomi, he well knew, did not understand his shed any more than she had understood the shed belonging to her ex and late husband, Cedric, and where he had, apparently, spent a considerable amount of time. Naomi maintained that he had spent it doing nothing but, in the Colonel's view, a man was entitled to do nothing or something in his own shed, just as he pleased. That was the whole point of it.

She said, 'Then you'll have plenty of room to spare for something useful.'

Naomi's dilapidated lean-to greenhouse was always full of useful things and her cottage windowsills were invariably crowded with an assortment of disposable containers and old yoghurt pots where she sowed seeds with her very green fingers.

'My shed is not up for discussion, Naomi.'

She shrugged. 'Fair enough. I'll never understand you men and your sheds.'

He said, as he had said to her before, 'You don't need to. The other half?'

She drained her glass. 'Don't mind if I do.'

He did the honours, added another log to the fire and went back to his wing chair. 'I'm wondering who's going to play the Snow Queen?'

'So am I. In the story she's tall, slender, dazzling and very beautiful. None of the female Frog End Players exactly fits that description. It would have been so much easier casting an ordinary panto where you've got men playing women and women playing men, and all the rest of it. I suppose Monica Pudsey could do it, at a pinch, but she's not tall, certainly not slender and there's nothing remotely dazzling about her.'

'Perhaps your make-up artist could work a miracle?'

'She'd need to.'

'How about a newcomer in the village? Someone who could be persuaded to join the Players?'

Naomi frowned. 'Unlikely. Most newcomers are as ancient as we are. Though there's a London couple who've just moved into Hassels. Haven't met them myself but I gather he's something on television. Kenneth Dryden. Rather well known, apparently. Used to do travel documentaries about faraway places like Kathmandu. I don't know what he does now. And apparently she was a famous model, once upon a time.'

'That's sounds promising.'

'If she's kept her looks. A lot of them go right off the boil, don't they? It's all to do with bone structure, so they say. If you've got good facial bones the skin's got something to hang on to. I think that's the general theory.'

'She'd also need to be able to act.'

'Not really. Most of the Players can't act for toffee. So long as she looks the part from a safe distance.' Naomi suddenly slapped her knee hard and Thursday jumped and glared. 'Tell you what, Hugh, I've just had a jolly good idea.'

'Oh?' Naomi's ideas had a habit of unsettling him.

'You go and call on the new people. See what she's like.'

'Me? Why me?'

'You're a man, aren't you? You'll know at once whether she could pass muster, or not.'

He said, 'You're seriously suggesting that I call on these people like some sort of casting agent, in order to decide whether the lady of the house would be right to play the Snow Queen?'

'That's right.'

'And am I supposed to offer her the part if she looks satisfactory?'

'No, we'll leave that to Marjorie. You'll just be welcoming them to the village. Showing them what nice people we are. Being neighbourly.'

'They're not exactly my neighbours.'

'Close enough.'

'And I'm a new boy myself.'

'Not any longer. You're a respected pillar of the community now, Hugh, as well as an old soldier. Just the one for the job. You mustn't let us down. Once more unto the breach, and so forth.'

'I don't see the Agincourt connection. Has it occurred to you, Naomi, that this lady might not be the slightest bit interested in the Frog End Players' Christmas offering, let alone taking part in it?'

'Marjorie is very persuasive, Hugh.'

She wasn't the only one, he thought. 'I'm not convinced that it's a sound idea.'

'It's our only idea at the moment. The success or failure of the Frog End Christmas play lies in your hands.'

'Hardly.'

'Yes, it does. You can be very charming, Hugh. I've seen you in action. You'll be able to convince her if anybody can.'

He had never thought of himself as charming. 'I very much doubt it.'

'That's precisely your charm. You don't realize you've got it. Come on, Hugh. Do it for Frog End, if for nothing else. You owe it to us.'

He knew it was true. Frog End had given him a new lease of life when he had almost given up on the old. 'When do you want me to call on them?'

'Tomorrow.'

THREE

The house called Hassels was on the other side of the village. It was built of stone with large, symmetrical windows, a slate roof and a porticoed front door. It was a cut above the poky cottages huddled round the village green like the Colonel's Pond Cottage, and about two hundred years younger.

He admired its uncluttered appearance. No beetle-browed thatch, no crooked beams, no lopsided little windows. The door was glossy white with brass fittings, the knocker heavy under his hand.

A girl opened the door about a foot wide and peered round the edge. She was a teenager with long fair hair hanging in a tangle round her face, framing a teenager's sulky expression.

'Yes?'

He said pleasantly, 'I wonder if Mr and Mrs Dryden are at home?'

She turned her head away and shouted over her shoulder, 'Dad! There's a man here to see you.'

'Who is it?'

'No idea.'

The girl disappeared and he waited in the porch until the door was opened wider by a man. He looked to be in his late fifties and was wearing a suede jacket and clothes of a style and quality rarely seen in Frog End. Something on television, Naomi had said. Used to do travel documentaries. Quite well known. The name was unfamiliar, and so was the face, but then the Colonel, like Naomi, watched very little television and was hopelessly out of touch in that respect, not to mention the many years spent abroad.

He introduced himself, apologising for the disturbance. The response was brusque and not encouraging.

'I'm Kenneth Dryden. You'd better come in, Colonel, though

it's not an ideal time. We're still in complete chaos, as you can see. Most of this stuff has been in storage for years.'

The hall was full of packing cases and he could sympathize, remembering the trauma of moving his worldly possessions from storage oblivion in Harrods Depository after he had sold the London flat. Things long forgotten and some that he could have sworn that he had never seen before had come to light. Furniture that had been passed on by his late mother-in-law and unwieldy or unnecessary items that had been left behind as he and Laura had moved from one army posting to another. Sorting it all out and getting rid of things that there had been no room for in Pond Cottage had been a nightmare.

The girl was on her way up the stairs.

Her father bellowed after her. 'Ask your mother to come down, Clarissa.'

'She's having a bath.'

'Well, she can come down as soon as she's finished it.'

'She'll take ages. She always does.'

'Tell her from me to bloody well hurry up.'

The drawing-room windows were draped with lengths of different fabrics – all looked very expensive. Heavy books of wallpaper samples lay open like mantraps on the floor, paint colour cards scattered around.

Kenneth Dryden said, 'Joan's got some fancy interior designer who's left all this stuff. Of course, she changes her mind all the time.'

'It's her prerogative, I believe.'

'Hmm. I've never understood why women can't make up their minds and stick to it. I could do with a drink if I can find some. How about you?'

It was only twenty past eleven, but so what? He'd been sent on a tricky mission which could take some time to complete. Kenneth Dryden produced a bottle of Laphroaig and glasses from a cupboard. Naomi would have been mightily impressed.

'Say when.'

He said it at the quarter full mark.

'Are you the official village welcomer, Colonel?'

'Far from it. I haven't lived here very long myself. But if you have any questions, I might know some of the answers.'

'I've no doubt we will have, once we think of them. English villages are something new to me. I've spent most of my life in a flat in London or travelling to remote places all over the world. You've probably seen some of my old TV programmes.'

'Indeed.' A useful word which meant almost nothing on its own.

'The bastards decided not to commission any more of them. It's always the bloody ratings, you see. That's all that counts these days. Everything dumbed down for the masses whose idea of travel is a package holiday or some unspeakable cruise. Everything done for them. Hand held every step of the way. Non-stop eating and entertainment. I imagine you're retired, Colonel?'

'For some time.'

'How long have you lived here?'

'Getting on for two years. I have a cottage on the green.'

'What do you make of Frog End? It looks a bit quiet to me. As though nothing much ever happens here.'

He smiled. 'I wouldn't say that. There's quite a lot going on, in fact. Talks in the village hall, jumble sales, coffee mornings, film shows, yoga classes, art classes, a gardening club, a bridge club – all kinds of clubs, in fact. Then there's the annual summer fête held at the Manor and, of course, the Frog End Players.'

'Who the hell are they?'

'The local amateur dramatic society. They put on two plays a year in the village hall. One in the summer, one at Christmas.'

'It's not compulsory to attend, I hope.'

Naomi's hopes were going to be dashed, the Colonel thought. 'Not at all.'

'Thank God for that. It was Joan's idea to get a place in the country, not mine. She likes the idea of having people down from London at weekends and dressing up in Barbours and Wellingtons – rather like Marie Antoinette playing at being a simple shepherdess. She was a rather famous model in her day, you know. Joan Lowe. I expect you've heard of her.'

'Indeed.' Once again, the useful word came to the rescue.

'Of course, we're keeping the flat in London and we'll still spend most of our time there.'

A telephone started ringing from somewhere and Kenneth Dryden eventually located it by the fireplace. The Colonel, to whom phone conversations still remained private affairs, moved tactfully away and stood looking out of a window at the winter scene of dormant plants and bare-branched trees. A silver birch provided the only highlight, its bark glistening white even on the dull grey day. No sign yet of any snowdrops emerging.

The phone conversation seemed to be finishing and he turned round to see a woman coming into the room.

'I gather we have a visitor, Kenny.'

'The Colonel has come to welcome us to Frog End, darling.'

'How kind of him.'

She came forward, her hand extended palm down and he took it in his, wondering if he was perhaps meant to kiss it. The nails, he noticed, were unpolished, the clothes artfully country casual. Marie Antoinette at play, as her husband had put it. She would probably be in her late forties but there was no evidence of her going off the boil, like Naomi had feared. She was still a very beautiful woman, tall and blonde, and with the glacial quality that often accompanies perfection. An ideal Snow Queen.

Freda Butler had observed the Colonel from the sitting-room window of Lupin Cottage as he had walked across the village green. She had tracked his progress and direction through the pair of powerful Zeiss binoculars which had been bequeathed to her when her father, the Admiral, had died. They had apparently belonged to a U-boat commander in the Second World War, though she was unsure how they had ended up in her father's possession since he had only sailed a desk in wartime. Indeed, they had only come into hers by the chance of discovering them in a drawer of the old bureau, left to her by default. The remainder of his estate, including a large oil portrait of the Admiral, together with his uniform and his medals, had been willed to a naval museum. Fortunately, the binoculars had not been mentioned in the will and she had decided not to mention them either.

She had watched the Colonel's straight-backed, soldier's

bearing with admiration, and the way he strode along so purposefully. If he had been a total stranger, she would have known that he was a military gentleman, even though he had been retired for a number of years. Once a soldier, always a soldier. And he was very handsome, she thought. Tall and silver-haired and lean – not gone to seed like some men of his age.

Miss Butler had served in the WRNS herself – an admittedly undistinguished career, unlike her father's – and the navy had been her whole life until retirement. But, to her mind, there was something about a soldier. Even the Major carried himself well – unless, of course, he was returning from the Dog and Duck.

She had kept the Colonel in her sights until he had disappeared out of range, presumably to pay a call on someone in the village. It was hard not to feel a little twinge of envy. The Colonel had been kindness itself to her, comforting her during a very unhappy and unfortunate patch of her life and respecting her confidence completely, not to mention helping her with the Red Cross collection, the Save the Donkey fund and the Help the Homeless cause. She knew that he was always exceedingly generous with his time when it came to doing things for other people and for the good of the village. They were very fortunate to have him. Not everyone was so willing to pull their weight. Of course, she and the Colonel shared a service background. He had paid a number of visits to Lupin Cottage to take a cup of tea, while she had been cordially invited into Pond Cottage, had sat in the sitting room and once quite informally in the kitchen so that she had been able to note his remarkable progress with the back garden, the terrace made with beautiful old flag stones, and the new shed.

The shed was a bit of a puzzle. It was rumoured that the Colonel spent a good deal of time in it, though nobody seemed to know quite what he did there, in spite of efforts to find out. Whatever it was, it was entirely his own business, so far as she was concerned, although it would be interesting to know.

She traversed the village green once more. It was not, she told herself, that she was spying on people, but her years in the WRNS had been spent involved in constant activity and in the company of other people. Retirement and living alone had left a void which could only partly be filled by charity work and village activities. Ironically, there were moments when she felt indebted to the unknown U-boat commander for providing her with, as it were, a new window on life; to be able to observe things so closely. She wondered sometimes what he had been like. What the U-boat crews had done had been terrible, she knew, but there was no denying their bravery. Very few of them had survived the war. The casualty figures were shocking.

On the third sweep, Mrs Bentley came into view, walking her four undisciplined and overweight dachshunds and, as usual, in danger of being tripped up by their leads. Miss Butler watched their chaotic progress: Mrs Bentley jerked this way and that, the dogs' leads encircling her ankles like maypole ribbons. Personally, she was not a dog lover, nor of cats who seemed to hold themselves aloof from humans. A case in point was the Colonel's moth-eaten old stray, Thursday, who had been given a good home but never showed the slightest bit of gratitude for it.

They were followed by Miss Rankin out exercising one of her riding school ponies and, after that, the vicar went by in his rather battered car, driving along the road round the edge of the green. He was a newcomer but seemed a very nice young man, though she would have preferred him without the beard. When he had first arrived he had had some unfortunate ideas, including a change in the old form and language of services. There were to be no more 'thee's' and 'thou's' and the ancient and beautiful words and phrases were to be replaced by up-to-date modern ones, said to be easier to understand. Naturally, there had been a great deal of opposition in the village. A positive storm of protest had soon put paid to the proposal. And a later plan to remove most of the pews to make space for community activities in the church nave, using stacking chairs instead, had been summarily torpedoed at a parish meeting; as ruthlessly, Miss Butler thought, as her U-boat commander would have dispatched his quarry to the bottom of the ocean. The poor vicar, so bewildered and confused that she had felt quite sorry for him, had seen the error of his ways and everyone had settled back into a normal routine.

The binoculars were heavy to hold and she unhooked them from round her neck and laid them carefully down on the table, straightening her navy blue cardigan. She always wore navy. Her time in the WRNS had left her feeling uncomfortable in any other colours.

It was a little early for lunch but she felt rather peckish. On her way to the small kitchen at the back of the cottage she passed by the bureau with the studio portrait of the Admiral on the top. Miss Butler avoided her father's stern and implacable gaze. Sometimes it was better not to be reminded of the disappointment she had been to him. A daughter, not a son. A failure, not a success.

Lunch was roes on toast. Not one of her favourites, especially since she had discovered what they were, but they were cheap and easy. When she had finished and washed up she went back to the sitting room and picked up the binoculars again. As luck would have it, she had timed her resumed watch with the Colonel's return. He was walking back across the green towards Pond Cottage and she saw him go up the path, unlock the front door and disappear inside. Within minutes, Naomi Grimshaw had come out of her cottage and was hammering on the Colonel's door.

'Well, Hugh, what was she like? Will she do?'

He'd been hanging his coat up in the hall and when he went to open the front door, Naomi almost fell inside.

'She certainly has the looks. Her professional name as a model was Joan Lowe.'

'Doesn't ring any bells with me.'

'Nor me. But, in any case, I don't think she'd consider the part for a moment.'

'Why not?'

'They've kept their flat in London and, according to her husband, they'll only be down here for the weekends. I wouldn't count on her joining the Frog End Players. Or anything else.'

'You can't be sure of that, Hugh.'

'No, I can't,' he agreed. 'It's just my impression.'

Rather a strong one, in fact. Joan Dryden had struck him as a woman who might find village life amusing, but only from a safe distance.

'Marjorie's planning to call on them and you know what she's like.'

'I do, indeed.'

'If she thinks Mrs Dryden's the ticket, she won't give up easily.'

'I don't think Mrs Dryden will either.'

His conversation with her had been perfectly pleasant but he had been aware that during it Joan Dryden had been assessing him – deciding whether he was worth bothering with or should be shown the door as quickly as possible. He must have passed the preliminary test because, after a while, he was invited to sit down and the paint colour cards were removed to make the necessary space on a sofa. He had even been asked to volunteer an opinion on a shade of grey-green that was apparently under consideration for the drawing room.

'What do you think of this one, Colonel? It's called Ashes.'

He had looked at the card she had held out in front of him. 'I'm afraid I'm no expert.'

His cottage walls had been painted throughout with magnolia emulsion. Laura had always chosen colours and materials and chosen extremely well. It was a knack, he knew, that some people had and others, like himself, did not. Joan Dryden would choose the most expensive ones, no doubt, but that was no guarantee of good taste. Sometimes it was the opposite.

'They say green's unlucky, don't they, Colonel? But I'm not superstitious. Are you?'

'Not generally.'

'Kenny doesn't like Ashes, do you, darling?'

'It's up to you, sweetie. Choose whatever you want.'

'On the other hand, we could have wallpaper instead.' She had indicated the mantraps on the floor. 'But I think paint would look better in this sort of room, don't you agree, Colonel?'

He had agreed. The well-proportioned room had seemed unsuited to anything fussy. It spoke for itself.

'And, of course, we could always have patterned curtains.' She had tweaked one of the sumptuous lengths draped at a window. 'What do you think of this one?'

'Very nice.'

'You don't sound sure, Colonel.'

'As I said, I'm no expert.'

The phone by the fireplace had started ringing again and Kenneth Dryden had snatched it up. A terse and exasperated conversation had followed. The Colonel had taken his cue and his leave. Joan Dryden had accompanied him to the front door.

'Poor Kenny. When he was making his travel documentaries he was left in peace to do things his own way. Now they're always on at him with their half-baked ideas. Have you seen his new programme?'

'I'm afraid not.'

'There's no reason why you should. It's on in the afternoons. The graveyard time. He talks to over-the-hill celebrities and boring nonentities, and the studio audience is made up of pensioners. It's been a bit of a shock to his system, not to mention his ego.'

'I'm sorry.'

'Well, it comes to us all, doesn't it? The slippery slope downhill.'

He had said gallantly and truthfully, 'I don't see much sign of it where you are concerned, Mrs Dryden.'

'Please call me Joan. You must come and see us again, Colonel. And bring your wife next time.'

'I'm a widower.'

'All the better.' She had held out her hand as regally as before. 'Well, it's been a pleasure to meet you, Colonel.'

He had walked away down the drive and when he reached the gateway he had glanced back to see her still standing in the doorway, watching him. She had waved to him, one arm gracefully uplifted, just like the Queen Mother used to do.

Naomi said, 'What did you talk about?'

'Not much. Mrs Dryden asked what I thought of a paint colour for the drawing-room walls.'

'You must have made a good impression.'

'Not necessarily. According to her husband, she always has great difficulty in making up her mind.'

'Well, let's hope Marjorie will be able to make it up for her.'

'Even she might have some difficulty with that.'

'I thought the Colonel was charming, Kenny. Almost an extinct species these days. Do you think there are any more like him in the village?

He shrugged. 'I've no idea.'

'He's a widower, you know. He'll be very useful to make up the numbers for dinner when we have people down.'

'Who's going to do the cooking for these country dinners?' Joan herself could barely make a cup of tea.

'I'll find someone.'

'They won't be up to London catering standards.'

'We'll keep things simple.'

'Let them eat cake, you mean?'

'What?'

Naturally, the Marie Antoinette allusion had escaped her.

'And how about cleaning this house?'

'Well, I won't be doing it, Kenny.'

'I'm aware of that.'

After nearly twenty years of marriage, Kenneth Dryden was well aware of most facts about his wife and one of these was that domesticity in any form was not in her make-up. It didn't worry him.

Or hadn't done while he had been making his travel documentaries and had been away for weeks, or even months, on end. In the early years she had been busy with her modelling – very successfully too. When he had first met her he had thought her one of the most beautiful women he had ever seen. She had knocked him for six. He'd regretted leaving his first wife, of course, but when he had set eyes on Joan everything had changed. All other women had paled into insignificance beside her and, in spite of the faults, later discovered, this remained true. He was no longer quite the star-struck lover of those early days but Joan was still in a class of her own and a big asset to him. People remembered her from her heyday. Joan Lowe was still a name to conjure with and it did his career no harm.

He said, 'Well, I'll leave all that side of things to you, darling. Just how often are you planning to have people down, as you put it?'

'Most weekends, I imagine.'

'There might be something to be said for having a bit of peace and quiet occasionally.'

'Kenny and Joan? The folks who live on the hill? You must be getting old, darling.'

The trouble was that he was. Next month he would be fifty-eight – nearly ten years older than Joan. The years spent travelling rough to the furthest corners of the earth had taken a toll and his afternoon TV show was taking even more of one, for different reasons. He hated doing it. He hated the pointless format. He hated the idiots who made it. He hated the dumb studio audience and, most of all, he hated the tenth-rate participants. None of this showed, of course. He was ever the genial, smiling host, ready with witty jokes and kindly encouragement. But it was a strain.

He said, 'It's bloody tiring doing the show. The batteries need recharging at weekends.'

'Well, you could always stay in London.'

'While you come down here?'

'It wouldn't worry me, Kenny. We've spent plenty of time apart, after all. I'm used to it. So are you.'

This was perfectly true but going away had been a neces-sary part of his work. He'd done it to earn a crust. Or more like the loaf it took to keep Joan in what she considered the vital necessities of life – a spare-no-expense apartment, designer clothes, must-be-seen-at restaurants and shows, exotic holidays and now the Marie Antoinette bucolic playhouse, apparently to be furnished on a Versailles scale. He had seen the eye-watering prices of the fabric samples lying around. And Clarissa wasn't cheap to run either, even though she dressed in rags. At the moment, it was driving lessons – an inordinate number of them, it seemed. Soon it would be a car, and not any old car. Only the newest and coolest would do. And new and cool invariably equalled expensive.

He had earned very good money with the documentaries but hardly vast Hollywood sums and the afternoon show did not pay nearly so well. Sometimes – but not often – he admitted to himself that he was in danger of becoming almost as much of a has-been as the forgotten celebrities on his show. If they gave him the chop, he didn't think he'd care – in fact, it would almost be a relief.

Except for the small matter of Joan. She was high-cost maintenance and he had to keep treading the wheel to provide for it. Somehow.

FOUR

'I've just been speaking on the telephone to Mrs Grimshaw, Roger.'

The Major poked gingerly at his lunch plate. Some kind of stew again, he supposed. Probably another recipe wrenched from a magazine at Marjorie's hairdresser's. Whatever kind it was, he couldn't identify any of the ingredients, though that chunk there might be carrot, or, God forbid, swede.

'What about?'

'The Colonel called on the new people at Hassels – Mr and Mrs Dryden.'

Had he, indeed? He wouldn't have put the Colonel down as such a fast worker – not at all the type to push himself forward, though there was no denying that he always seemed to make a good impression. Must be something to do with being an old soldier. Old soldiers were respected in society. He'd found that himself, as was only right when you'd served your country faithfully for years and put your life on the line. And, of course, the Colonel had kept his hair and all that sort of thing. He was tall, too. Not that height counted with women. Look at Napoleon, for instance – Josephine couldn't have cared less that he was on the short side. And Monty had been pretty small too, not that he'd ever been a ladies' man, by all accounts. Quite the opposite.

He said, 'I'm told Mrs Dryden was a fashion model once.'

'Who told you?'

'Can't remember. She was quite famous, apparently. Under another name.'

It was definitely swede, not carrot, he decided, testing the watery yellow chunk. Animal feed! He thought wistfully of the curries when they'd been in India and Malaya. By Jove, those chaps knew how to cook! The food actually tasted of something, not like this mush.

'Well, Naomi Grimshaw says that the Colonel thinks she might do for the Snow Queen.'

'What Snow Queen?'

'For heaven's sake, Roger! The Frog End Players' Christmas play. We talked about it, remember?'

He did, but not the details. Some silly fairy tale they were doing instead of a proper pantomime. Odd that the Colonel had got himself involved. Not his sort of thing, he'd have thought.

'Has she agreed?'

'We haven't asked her yet.'

He remembered the glimpse he had caught of Mrs Dryden when he'd been driving by in the Escort. Only a glimpse, but it had been enough to put him in the picture. He prided himself on knowing about women – could sum them up with one look.

'Doubt if she'd be interested.'

'Nonsense, Roger. The Drydens are new to the village so they'll be very keen to join in things. To be accepted. Besides, I'm going to call and ask her personally myself. She's bound to agree.'

He wasn't a betting man but if he had been, he'd have said that the odds were about even.

In Marjorie Cuthbertson's opinion, there was no time to lose. As soon as lunch finished, she left Roger to do the washing-up and walked briskly out of Shangri-La and the cul-de-sac in the direction of Hassels. Unlike the cul-de-sac bungalows, huddled cheek by jowl, the Georgian house stood on its own in two acres or more of land. Large but not too large. Far more manageable than Frog End Manor, for instance. She had always admired it. It was exactly the sort of place she would have wished to retire to, and would have done so if only Roger had made more of a success of his army career. Her father had been a Major General, after all, and although Roger had seemed promising enough when she had first met him as a keen young subaltern, it had to be said that he had turned out to be something of a disappointment.

Fortunately, she had had the sense to make the best of a poor situation and had adapted to retirement in a bungalow, deploying her own natural authority and her organizing capabilities in as many village affairs as possible. However, when she approached the front porch of Hassels and lifted the brass knocker, the regrets returned.

Her knock went unanswered. She waited for a few minutes and then used the knocker again, harder this time. It took a third knock, louder and firmer still, before the door was wrenched open by none other than Mr Dryden himself. She recognized him from his travel documentaries which she had occasionally watched when they had been home on leave, though he looked a good deal older in the flesh and smaller, too. Apparently, that was often the case. She thrust out her hand with a confident smile.

'I'm Marjorie Cuthbertson. Welcome to Frog End.'

He beckoned her inside – rather impatiently, she thought. Not quite what she was used to, but then manners had declined as other things had advanced. She stepped over the threshold. The previous owners had been quite unsociable and she had never actually seen the inside of the house. The hall was just the sort of spacious entrance that she would have liked and a far cry from the cramped passageway at Shangri-La. She could see herself greeting guests graciously here, and in the proper manner.

'I'm on the phone. Wait here, please.'

He disappeared, leaving her marooned among a sea of packing cases. As she waited, a girl came slouching down the staircase and passed her without a nod, let alone a smile. Really! She might have been completely invisible. Mr Dryden returned.

'I'm sooo sorry about that. Something I had to deal with rather urgently.' He was smiling a very charming smile. 'Would you mind telling me your name again?'

'Marjorie Cuthbertson.'

'Of course! It's kind of you to call, Mrs Cuthbertson. My wife, Joan, is in the drawing room, trying to decide between curtain fabrics. She'd be delighted to meet you.'

Mollified, she followed him into the room, which made the Shangri-La's sitting room seem even more inadequate than its hall. She noted that the girl who had passed her was now lying full length on a sofa, flicking through the pages of a magazine. She was wearing blue jeans that had frayed holes on both knees. Someone had once explained to her that this was intentional and that clothes manufacturers ripped holes in perfectly good cotton to make wearers look like tramps.

Kenneth Dryden said, 'This is Mrs Cuthbertson, darling. She's called to welcome us to Frog End.'

The woman standing over by the window was holding up a length of material at its edge. When she turned round Marjorie Cuthbertson saw that, for once, Roger might have been right about her having been a famous fashion model, and why the Colonel had considered her very possible for the Snow Queen. She had seen photographs of such women in magazines. Very glamorous. Very haughty. And wearing couture clothes that cost quite scandalous amounts of money. Fashion models used to be called mannequins in the old days, if she remembered rightly, and were considered a rather low form of life, whereas nowadays some of them seemed to have acquired exalted celebrity status, for what that was worth. Personally, she found it extraordinary that clothes should be given such importance. Their prime function, after all, was simply to cover you decently and to keep you warm or cool, depending on the weather. She herself had a useful stock of garments left over from the army years spent abroad in hot climates which still came in useful occasionally in England for what passed for summer. Otherwise, she dressed almost invariably in tweed skirts and woollen twin sets or polo neck jumpers, with a quilted gilet on top if necessary.

The woman had put down the length of material and came closer. No doubt about it, she looked and moved the part.

'How do you do. I'm Joan Dryden.'

The voice was right too. It matched the face. Ice cold and aloof. Better and better, Marjorie Cuthbertson thought to herself. She'll hardly have to act at all. She can just be herself. I might as well get straight to the point. No time to waste.

She said heartily, 'We could do with some new blood in the village, Mrs Dryden. Would you be interested in joining the Frog End Players? We're keen as mustard to get new members.'

'The Frog End Players?'

'Our amateur dramatic society. We put on two productions a year: one during the summer and another at Christmas. Although I say it myself, we're very professional. The local press always gives us a good write-up.'

Kenneth Dryden was smiling. 'I think you should join, darling. You'd get to know people.'

'I already know a great many people, thank you, Kenny.'

'But not in Frog End. Perhaps you'd be interested, too, Clarissa? You'd meet some of the young people round here.'

The girl lying on the sofa rolled her eyes. 'Spare me, Dad.' She went on flicking through the magazine pages.

Joan Dryden said, 'I'm afraid we'll have to disappoint you, Mrs Cuthbertson. I'm not interested in amateur dramatics, and nor is my daughter – as you can see. In any case, we'll be spending the greater part of our time in London.'

Marjorie Cuthbertson played her trump card, as she saw it.

'That's a great pity. We're looking for someone to play the starring role in our production this Christmas and I happen to think it might suit you extremely well.'

'Really?'

She plunged on regardless. 'You see, we're doing *The Snow Queen*!'

'The what?'

'*The Snow Queen*. The well-known fairy tale by Hans Christian Andersen which we've adapted for the stage. I think you'd be perfect as our queen.'

The Major was sure he could feel a sore throat coming on. Or perhaps it was flu? Whatever it was, it needed urgent attention. You couldn't be too careful at his age and that was a fact. He'd just finished reading the day's obituaries in the paper and there were two names he'd recognized. Chaps he'd known in the distant past.

With any luck, Marjorie wouldn't be back for a while from calling on the new people. Time enough for him to have a medicinal glass. Something to kill off the bugs before they took hold.

He got up from his armchair and went boldly over to the

cocktail cabinet. As he opened the lid 'Drink to Me Only With Thine Eyes' started up loudly but, with the old girl out of earshot, there was no need to worry. It could play away all it liked and he could take his time.

'Or leave a kiss within the cup
And I'll not ask for wine.
The thirst that from the soul doth rise
Doth ask a drink divine
But might I of Jove's nectar sip,
I would not change for thine.'

He hummed along as he poured himself a large one, big enough to do the trick, and had closed the lid and just sat down again when he heard the front door open. No time to drink even a sip. He hid the glass behind his armchair and was reading his newspaper when Marjorie strode in, making the ornaments rattle. When they'd been serving abroad the native servants had always entered a room softly and glided about without a sound. He remembered things like that fondly.

'How did you get on, dear?'

She sat down on the sofa, her feet planted apart. Marjorie's legs, encased in brown stockings, always made him think of the gateposts leading in to Shangri-La, though without the scrape marks.

'Very odd sort of set-up, I thought. Not the sort of thing we're used to. Mr Dryden was on the telephone for a very long time and there was a teenage daughter who had no manners at all. In fact, she was extremely rude.'

'What about the wife? Was she a model?'

'I didn't ask, but she certainly looked like she had been once.'

He lowered the newspaper further. 'Oh?'

'Don't get your hopes up, Roger. She wouldn't give you the time of day.'

'Nothing further from my mind.'

In fact, the hope was always at the front of it. A fading hope as the years passed in Frog End, but still lingering. He was not exactly in his prime, but he was not that far past it. There was plenty of life left in him yet. A jolly old flame has lots of sparks. Many a good tune was played on an old fiddle.

He said, 'Did you ask her about playing the part?'

'First I told her about the Frog End Players – to set the scene, as it were. Then I asked her if she'd like to join.'

'What did she say?'

'She wasn't remotely interested.'

'I didn't think she would be.'

'So then I told her that I thought she'd make a marvellous Snow Queen and that it would be the starring part in the play.'

The Major still had his doubts. 'What did she think about that?'

'She turned it down. Can you imagine? The starring part handed to her on a plate.'

He could imagine the scene very easily. 'Maybe she didn't see it that way.'

'Luckily, her husband was on my side. He told her how much her friends from London would love coming down to see her in a village play. I had the distinct impression that he thought it would be rather amusing for everyone. All jolly good fun. I'm not sure that he quite understood that *The Snow Queen* is a serious moral tale, not some frivolous pantomime.'

'So, what happened?'

'Well, I told her that she'd hardly have any lines to learn and that we would hire a very good costume for her as the star of the show and that there would only be three performances. In the end, she agreed. There's no need to look so surprised, Roger. I can usually make people change their minds, you know.'

The old girl went off to make a cup of tea in the kitchen, which gave him the chance to retrieve the glass from behind the chair and swallow the contents in a few gulps. He could feel it doing his throat good as it went down, and the rest of him perking up.

The news that Mrs Dryden was to play the Snow Queen had given him a much-needed boost. He wouldn't mind the scene-shifting nearly so much if she was going to be around.

FIVE

The Colonel had consulted an electrician about running a cable out to his shed. The man had come out from Dorchester and pronounced it a simple matter to arrange: 'No problem there, guv.' Within a few days the Colonel not only had lighting in the shed but also warmth from a heater. There was even an extra power point available should he need it.

He had decided that the time had definitely come to progress from plastic model kits to something more demanding – to some serious woodwork, if he was up to the challenge. Nails, screws, nuts and bolts he already had in abundance, ranged in jars on a shelf, as well as the basic carpentry hand tools kept in a partition at the end of the workbench. He had gone out to buy more tools – chisels, a plane, saws and a sanding block, as well as an electric drill and jigsaw. And he had bought an illustrated guide to *Using Woodwork Tools* and a very interesting book suggesting *Heirloom Wooden Toy Projects. You will be creating an heirloom*, the book had told him encouragingly. *One that can be handed down from generation to generation and treasured long after you've gone*, though he rather doubted that he could make anything of the kind. The book also said where to send for plans and step-by-step instructions. He had particularly liked the picture of a toddler's rocking horse. It was a very simple shape with big holes for eyes, smaller ones for nostrils and a frayed rope tail. It might please his new granddaughter, Edith, and it should also please his daughter-in-law, being low and sturdy with safe grab handles on each side of the horse's head. With luck, it might be ready in time for Christmas. Later, he would have to think of something suitable to make for Eric. Perhaps a chess set, also pictured in the book. Five wasn't too young to learn and he would take pleasure in teaching him. After all, it was a game closely related to the one they had played with his old tin soldiers on the sitting-room carpet when Eric had come to stay on his own. Battle formations, tactics, manoeuvres, outflanking and encirclement. Surprise attack, counter-attack, advance, retreat, capture and, finally, surrender. Checkmate!

He sent for the plans which arrived within a few days, enclosing the promised instructions. A trip to a helpful local lumber yard provided him with suitable wood. He was ready to start.

He began by cutting out the paper patterns which he laid out on the wood, taping them in place and, as instructed, paying special attention to the section that would make the horse's head. The aim was to find an interesting and flowing grain that would represent the speed of a running horse.

He started with the head, tracing carefully round the pattern edges on to the wood with a biro. He had just reached the tip of the horse's ear and started down towards the nose and mouth when there was a loud knocking on the shed door. His first thought was that it was Naomi. Luckily, the sacking curtains were up at the windows and, if he stayed perfectly still, there was just a faint possibility that she would go away. More knocking – this time louder and urgent. Impossible to ignore. He went to unlock and open the door.

It wasn't Naomi. Marjorie Cuthbertson stood there, gloved hand raised to rap yet again.

'I thought you must be here, Colonel. When I tried the cottage, there was no answer.'

He wondered how he could ever have imagined himself safe from callers and interruptions when it was probable that the entire village knew about his shed at the bottom of the garden. There was no chance whatever of her going away and a woman of her size and shape would be hard to deflect once her mass started moving forwards. He stepped outside the shed, shutting and locking the door firmly behind him; a manoeuvre he often used with Naomi. Unfortunately it was starting to rain.

'Perhaps we should go inside?'

He led the way into the cottage, through the kitchen and into the sitting room where Thursday was asleep in his place on the sofa. The log fire was unlit as yet, but fortunately the central heating had come on. Mrs Cuthbertson, he knew, always maintained that she had never been able to re-adapt properly to the English climate after so many years spent in the tropics.

'Please sit down.'

Thursday had opened his eyes to glittering slits and the Colonel watched as Mrs Cuthbertson lowered herself on to the sofa beside him. As she went down, Thursday went up.

'So, this is your stray cat. I've heard all about him. It looks as though he's fallen on his feet.'

Mrs Cuthbertson stretched out a gloved hand towards the black-and-tan lump of fur and the Colonel held his breath. To his amazement, Thursday remained in situ and graciously allowed himself to be stroked, even to have the underside of his chin rubbed and his torn ear tickled.

Mrs Cuthbertson said, 'We always had cats when I was a child. I prefer them to dogs. Dogs are too slavish, in my opinion. Roger doesn't agree, of course.'

Therein lay the reason for Thursday's amenable behaviour. Mrs Cuthbertson was a cat person. She came straight to the point, as she usually did.

'I've come to recruit you, Colonel. The Frog End Players need your help with our Christmas play.'

'I'm afraid I'm no good at acting.'

'We've got plenty of members who aren't either. We're not asking you to do any acting. What we always need are volunteers to help with scene-shifting. There's a shortage of strong, able-bodied men in the village, as you may have noticed.'

Her eye was fixed upon him and he could see that she was ready to deal with any lame excuse, even if he could think one up.

'I'd be glad to help.'

'Jolly good! And I have another special favour to ask.'

He braced himself. 'Oh?'

'As you know, we're doing *The Snow Queen* – rather a departure from our usual Christmas entertainment. Are you familiar with the story, Colonel?'

'Only the general gist.'

'It's rather a complicated tale but we intend to simplify it – to strip it down to the essentials so that it's easier for the children to understand. Good triumphing over evil – as in a

pantomime, of course – but without any of the vulgarity, I'm
glad to say. Fortunately, I was able to persuade Mrs Dryden,
whom I gather you've met, to take the starring role of the
Snow Queen.'

He wondered if Joan Dryden was aware that she would be
playing Evil Incarnate.

'I'm sure it will be a great success.'

'Our productions usually are. The village appreciates our
efforts. We make all our own costumes – except for the ones
for the leading roles, which we hire. We also provide our own
scenery and it's all hands to the pumps when it comes to
painting backdrops. Everyone mucks in to help. It's all done
on a shoestring. We rather pride ourselves on that. People are
surprisingly good at contriving all kinds of props out of whatever bits and pieces they can find. Very resourceful. That's
rather where you come in, Colonel.'

He said cautiously, 'How, exactly?'

'The story begins in summer when the roses and other
flowers are blooming but then winter comes with snow and
ice heralding the arrival of the Snow Queen. It's quite a challenge for our scenic skills.'

'It must be, indeed.'

'We can make the summer flowers out of paper and, for
winter, we plan to have a large backdrop of snow-capped
mountains with some real Christmas trees planted in buckets
to give depth to the scene. Flora Bentley has had the inspired
idea of spraying the trees with silver glitter on the one side
and leaving the other green so that we can just turn them round
to change summer to winter as the story progresses. Awfully
clever, don't you think?'

'Very.'

'We were wondering if you would make us a wooden sledge.'

'A sledge?'

'Yes, a sledge. You know, for going over snow.'

He thought of the heirloom rocking horse painstakingly
traced past the ear and heading for the nose, and of his hope
and intention of finishing it by Christmas. The pattern pieces
would have to be cut out with a saw and sanded smooth, the
horse's legs trimmed at an exact angle, holes drilled, glue

applied, wooden dowels fitted and hammered home, the rockers assembled very accurately, the tail made and so on. The design was very simple but the instructions were not. There was a long way to go.

'I'm afraid I'm a complete beginner at carpentry, Mrs Cuthbertson. It would be rather beyond me.'

She wagged a playful finger. 'Come now, Colonel, you're being much too modest. I hear that you have a wonderful set of tools in your shed. It's for the Snow Queen, you see. There's a dramatic scene where she passes by on her sledge and steals the boy, Kai. We only need something simple that she and the boy can sit on and be pulled across the stage at the end of a rope. Nothing elaborate. A few planks nailed together, painted white. I'm sure you could manage that quite easily.'

Defeat was staring him in the face and he knew it. Edith's rocking horse would have to be set aside to make way for the Snow Queen's sledge.

'I'll do my best, Mrs Cuthbertson.'

'I knew you wouldn't let us down, Colonel. It would need concealed wheels underneath, of course, or we'd never be able to move it with Mrs Dryden and the boy on it when she carries him off to her ice palace at the North Pole.'

He was thankful that Mrs Cuthbertson wouldn't be on the sledge as well. 'I'll work something out.'

'Excellent! In the story, of course, it's actually a horse-drawn sleigh and we'd thought of asking Phillipa Rankin to let us borrow her Shetland pony to pull it, but the stage is too small and you can never rely on live animals to behave in public, can you?'

He pictured the possible scene. 'It could be unfortunate.'

'Quite so. We've had to lower our sights and go for a pull-along sledge. We have our first read-through next Tuesday at the village hall, starting at seven thirty p.m. sharp. I think it would be helpful for you to come along so that you can get a general idea of things. Thereafter, we rehearse every Tuesday evening at the same time and on Sunday afternoons at two p.m. As a non-Player, you won't be required to attend all of them, but I would appreciate the sledge being finished and ready in time to practise with it at the final rehearsals. Now, I really must toddle.'

She rose to her feet and gave Thursday another stroke, sweeping confidently from head to tail. He stretched out a claw-sheathed paw to indicate traitorous approval.

'I did warn you about her, Hugh.'

'Not enough.'

'Well, it's only a sledge. And you've got nothing else particular to work on at the moment, have you?'

He had no intention of mentioning the heirloom rocking horse. Naomi would certainly want to see it and finger the parts. She was not being in the least sympathetic about the sledge and he had a deep suspicion that she was responsible for the whole village, including Marjorie Cuthbertson, knowing the contents of his shed. The ignoble idea crossed his mind to pour her a smaller whisky than usual, but he resisted it. Thursday, after all, had been given full supper rations in spite of his blatant treachery.

She raised her glass to him. 'Cheers, Hugh. Perhaps I can help? Hold things for you? Do something?'

It was out of the question for Naomi to be given free and unlimited access to the shed.

He said firmly, 'No, thank you.'

'I've got an old wooden pallet you could have. I had some bricks delivered on it years ago.'

'Do you also have a fairy wand to turn it into a sledge?'

'You won't need one. The village boys always used to make sledges out of pallets when it snowed.'

'Would you mind telling me how?'

'With pleasure. It's easy. First, you make the pallet narrower by sawing through the struts holding the top boards in place.' Naomi made sawing movements in the air with her free hand. 'That gives you your platform. Then you separate out three boards from the leftover chunk and cut a curve across their ends to use as runners. After that, you nail the runners, on edge, to the underside of the pallet with the curved bits sticking out at the front. All you need is a bit of rope and, Bob's your uncle, you've got a sledge.'

'Fit for a queen?'

'Good enough. Improvisation is the name of the game with the Frog End Players. It's amazing what can be done. You'll paint it, of course?'

'White – so I've been instructed. Mrs Cuthbertson also wants concealed wheels so that it can be pulled across the stage. How do you suggest I conjure up those?'

'Ask Steph. He'll think of something.'

'You mean Steve, as was?'

'He's your man – or woman.'

Some time ago, the burly and tattoo-armed mechanic at the local garage had let it be known that in future he would like to be known as Steph, short for Stephanie. The Colonel had been happy to oblige. Steve, or Steph, had done some first-class work on the Riley and what he wished to be called was immaterial. By any other name he was still a fantastic mechanic. Apart from taking to wearing bright-coloured jumpsuits instead of greasy grey overalls, a gold ring in one ear and his hair in a ponytail, there was otherwise no difference.

'If you come round sometime, Hugh, I'll show you the pallet. It doesn't look much at the moment, but don't let that worry you.'

'I'll try not to,' he said.

Later, when Naomi had gone, he took out one of his old Gilbert and Sullivan records, set it on the player turntable and pressed the switch. The mere action of doing so was soothing and satisfying. Alison had tried, unsuccessfully, to convert him to compact discs, but he liked his vinyl records: they were faithful friends, collected over many years, and he knew every word of every song. As he listened, beating the time with his hand on the chair arm, his irritation ebbed away.

'In enterprise of martial kind,
When there was any fighting,
He led his regiment from behind –
He found it less exciting.
But when away his regiment ran,
His place was at the fore, O –
That celebrated,
Cultivated,

Underrated
Nobleman,
The Duke of Plaza-Toro.'
Naomi's pallet sledge just might work. It should certainly
be strong – after all, pallets were designed to bear heavy
weights – and what it lacked in looks could be made up for
with several coats of white paint. Perhaps even a spray of
some of Flora Bentley's Christmas tree glitter? In any case,
he doubted that the audience would take too much notice of
the conveyance. All eyes would be on the Snow Queen.

SIX

Frog End village hall had been built in 1863 when Queen Victoria sat firmly on the throne. It was a solid, red-brick building made to last for many years and well designed for its intended purpose – a place for use by the villagers. The Colonel had been there on numerous occasions – to jumble sales, coffee mornings and bridge evenings, to lectures and talks on all manner of subjects, including his own (reluctantly delivered) about his army days. Residents often gave talks about their holiday travels, usually accompanied by a large number of slides which tended to be projected upside down or in the wrong order. He had sailed up the Amazon and down the Nile, journeyed along the canals of England, visited the Great Wall of China, plumbed the depths of the Great Barrier Reef, admired the Taj Mahal, the Pyramids and the Northern Lights, and all without moving from a chair in the hall. The days when people spent their whole life in one village, rarely venturing beyond its boundaries, were long gone. The labourers, blacksmiths, bakers, woodmen, gamekeepers and domestic servants had vanished, together with the village carpenter who had made coffins, acted as undertaker, and had also, as an added service, written wills and letters in fine copperplate handwriting. Today, only a handful of elderly people had been born in Frog End and stayed. Residents had come from other places and still kept in touch with the outside world – as demonstrated by the far-ranging travel talks.

The Colonel escorted Naomi across the green to the village hall, shining a torch ahead of them to light the way. It was a quarter to seven when they arrived and it looked as though most of the Players were already present with Mrs Cuthbertson in full command, directing operations with outstretched arms like a policeman controlling traffic. A trestle table had been dragged out and set up below the stage and chairs were being unstacked and placed around it, others arranged in a concentric row at a distance.

'The speaking parts sit at the table for the read-through,' Naomi told him. 'The rest of us lesser mortals listen from a respectful distance and try not to fall asleep.'

Mrs Bentley approached, looking triumphant. 'I see you changed your mind about us, Colonel. You'll be surprised at how much you'll enjoy yourself.'

He would, indeed.

The Major was wrestling with two chairs that refused to be parted from each other and he went to give him a hand.

'Didn't expect to see you here, Colonel. Not your cup of tea, I'd have thought. Not mine either, I can tell you.'

They managed to unlock the chairs and add them to the end of the row.

The Major wiped his brow with his handkerchief. 'Some damned silly fairy tale they're doing this year. That weedy-looking fellow standing over there has done the script. Apparently he wrote a book about something once. Never read it, of course. Don't tell me Marjorie's persuaded you to tread the boards?'

'No, just scene-shifting and a bit of carpentry.'

'Carpentry? Didn't know that was your thing.'

The Major must be the only one in the village who didn't know about the shed.

'I'm a complete beginner.'

'Well, you have to start somewhere, I suppose. What's Marjorie got you doing?'

'Making a sledge for the Snow Queen.'

'By Jove, that's rather a tall order.' The Major moved closer and gave him a nudge with his elbow. 'I hear you met Mrs Dryden. Quite a looker, isn't she? Used to be a famous model, you know.'

'So I understand.'

'Husband's a TV personality, or whatever you call them?'

'I believe so.'

The Major looked across at his wife. He sighed. 'Some people have all the luck.'

The Colonel went on making himself useful, carrying more

chairs and taking one from Miss Butler who was struggling with it gamely.

'How kind of you, Colonel! Thank you so much. They're such awkward things to handle, I find.' She thanked him several more times, trotting after him across the hall. 'Are you a new member of the Players?'

'No. Just a helper.'

'That's all I am, really. I don't act but I help with the costumes and props. We have to make most of them ourselves, you see. It's all done on a shoestring, though I expect they'll be hiring a professional costume for the Snow Queen, it being the main part. I understand you've already met Mr and Mrs Dryden.'

'Very briefly.'

'I haven't liked to call on them yet, myself. I'm sure they're very nice.'

He made some non-committal reply.

Miss Butler said, 'We're not used to having celebrities in Frog End, are we, Colonel? Except for Miss Delaney, of course, and she wasn't here for long.'

Lois Delaney, star of the London stage many years ago, had moved into one of the new flats converted from Naomi's old childhood home. The actress had died in her bath, electrocuted by her hairdryer. The Colonel, asked by Miss Butler to go round the village collecting for the Save the Donkey fund, had been the one to find her. He had also been present when Lady Swynford had been discovered dead in her bed during the summer fête held at the Manor, and last spring he had been summoned by an old friend when builders had unearthed an inconvenient skeleton in her barn. More recently, he had attended an RAF Bomber Command reunion in Lincolnshire where the mid-upper gunner of a former Lancaster crew had been drowned in an unfortunate boating incident.

As Naomi had somewhat caustically remarked, he always seemed to be getting mixed up with dead bodies.

She came up to him now, another woman in tow. 'Hugh, this is Thora Jay, our make-up artist. Remember my telling you about her? She can make anyone look good.'

Naomi had described her as fading into the background, and said that nobody would notice her. He certainly had no recollection of ever having met her before. She was somewhere in her middle sixties, he judged – a small, thin, colourless woman with unremarkable features. It was hard to imagine her performing make-up miracles on others.

He smiled at her. 'I shouldn't think you'll have too much trouble with the Snow Queen.'

She said, 'You can never tell, Colonel. I can make plain women look beautiful if they're nice people, but it's not always so easy otherwise.'

He looked at her more closely. Unnoticeable she might seem, but certainly not unintelligent. Or dull. He said, 'Have you met Mrs Dryden?'

'Not yet.'

'Well, she should be here soon.'

'I'm looking forward to it.'

Mrs Bentley accosted him again. 'Having a good time, Colonel?'

'Indeed.' Yet again, the useful word came to his rescue.

'You seem to be entering into the spirit of things, Colonel. I hear that you're making us a beautiful sleigh for the Snow Queen.'

A sleigh conjured up the vision of an elegant conveyance being drawn across deep snow by nodding horses, their manes flowing, harness bells jingling. Or perhaps Father Christmas and his reindeer soaring through the star-studded night sky, laden with toys. It had nothing to do with Naomi's old wooden pallet.

'Just an ordinary sledge, I'm afraid.'

'Well, I'm sure you'll do a wonderful job. I hear you're always hard at work in that shed of yours. How's it coming along?'

'I haven't actually started yet.'

She dug her fingers into his arm. 'You'd better get a move on, Colonel. Time and tide wait for no man.'

Nor did Marjorie Cuthbertson. He saw how she kept checking her watch. Two minutes to seven but no sign of the Snow Queen. Five more minutes passed and Mrs Cuthbertson clapped her hands.

'Take your places, please.'

Flora Bentley said, 'But shouldn't we wait for Mrs Dryden?'

'I'll read her part until she arrives.'

They were well into the opening scene before Joan Dryden made her entrance into the hall, accompanied by her husband. The evil sorcerer, inventor of the magic mirror, being played with relish by Mr Rix, a retired dentist, was cut off in mid-cackle.

Mrs Cuthbertson rose to her feet. 'We're so glad you could join us, Mrs Dryden. Your place is at the far end of the table, if you would please sit down. You'll find your copy of the script there.'

The Snow Queen took her time. Space had to be made for her consort and another chair fetched. The long and luxurious fur coat that she was wearing – rather a departure from the simple Marie Antoinette theme – was taken off and then quickly retrieved as the temperature in the hall struck home. Somebody pointed out the place in the script for her and spectacles had to be found in the depths of a large black handbag, necessitating a search to the very bottom and most of the contents being taken out and piled on the table in the process.

Eventually, Mrs Cuthbertson sat down again. 'Proceed, Mr Rix.'

The sorcerer resumed his manic cackling. 'How clever am I to have constructed this mirror. It is not an ordinary mirror that you see before you. This is a magic mirror. A very peculiar mirror. It makes every beautiful thing look ugly, every good person look evil. Come closer and gaze into its depths. Let its power take over.' More cackling. 'If it should ever break, billions and trillions of splinters would fly about the world and lodge in people's eyes and in their hearts. With this mirror, Evil will conquer the world!'

Yet more cackling. The Major was muttering something beneath his breath.

Three long hours later, the Colonel escorted Naomi back across the green.

'Well, what did you think of her, Hugh?'

'Who?'

'Our Snow Queen, of course.'

'She should be rather good. She only has to be herself.'

'Very true. And she'll certainly look the part, especially by the time Thora's worked her magic. Monica Pudsey's very put out at not being given the role. Marjorie offered her the wise old Lapland woman instead but she turned it down flat. Did you notice how she was sulking this evening?'

'I can't say I did.'

'Anyway, she would have been hopeless. That fur coat Joan Dryden was wearing was the real thing, you know. Nothing faux about it. Real, genuine wolf – like my great uncle's Cossack hat.'

'I thought I recognized the fur.'

Naomi had a striking assortment of headgear that had belonged to various long-dead members of her family. The hats were kept in an old tin trunk in her attic and if a suitable occasion occurred she would take one out to wear it. Great Aunt Rosalind's magnificent Edwardian flower and feather creation, for instance, had made a dramatic appearance at Ruth and Tom's wedding last summer. And a very impressive grey wolf Cossack soldier's hat, appropriated by a great uncle who had fought in a cavalry regiment, had been brought out several times during a recent cold spell.

He had noted Joan Dryden's fur coat, glaringly out of place in the village hall, but he had been paying more attention to its wearer, calculating her weight and that of the boy playing the part of Kai who was to be carried off by the Snow Queen to her icy palace at the North Pole. The sledge would have to be big enough and strong enough to take them both.

Naomi had apparently divined his thoughts. 'That old pallet of mine is still waiting for you, Hugh – unless you've thought of a better idea.'

He had, in fact, been studying a sledge illustrated in his book of *Heirloom Wooden Toy Projects*, but it was designed for a small child, made from fine quality wood and intended to last for generations, whereas the one for the Snow Queen would only be needed for three performances.

He said, 'I'll come over in the morning to collect it, if that's all right with you.'

Naomi echoed Mrs Bentley. 'The sooner you get on with it the better.'

Miss Butler decided to make herself a cup of Ovaltine to settle herself before she went up to bed. She had found the read-through very tiring. Mrs Cuthbertson had interrupted the proceedings many times – in fact, the only person she had not interrupted had been Mrs Dryden who, in Miss Butler's own opinion, had been far from perfect as the Snow Queen.

In many ways, Mrs Dryden reminded her of the late Lady Swynford of Frog End Manor, who had come to such an unfortunate end during the summer fête. It was very un-Christian to think so, but Miss Butler privately considered that it had served her right. She had disliked Ursula Swynford intensely. She had been an arrogant and vain woman with a habit of ignoring people whom she had felt beneath her notice. She had simply looked through them as though they didn't exist. Miss Butler had experienced this treatment frequently and with much resentment. She, after all, had been an Admiral's daughter, while Ursula Swynford's parents, as she had later discovered, had been nothing special at all. Her diction had also been affected, but it had been acquired, whereas Mrs Dryden's, to give her her due, was real.

A cluster of people had gathered around the Drydens at the end of the read-through – moths drawn to a flame. It had not been possible to introduce herself but it seemed likely that, if she had, Mrs Dryden would have responded to her in exactly the same sort of way as Lady Swynford.

Freda Butler sipped her Ovaltine. She wished very much that the Drydens had not come to live in the village. In her view, they were bound to cause nothing but trouble.

The Major made no bones about heading straight for a nightcap on their return to Shangri-La. By God, he'd earned it! He hoped that Marjorie would go off to bed and leave him in peace, but she didn't.

'I think that went rather well this evening, Roger. Don't you agree?'

His opinion was rarely asked and he knew better than to give it. 'Absolutely. First rate.'

'One or two teething problems but I'll get them straightened out. Mr Rix needs to be toned down and Mrs Simcocks turned up – I could hardly hear a word she was saying and the kindly grandmother is a leading part. Quite crucial. Mrs Dryden was excellent, though, don't you think?'

He'd fallen asleep several times during the evening but woken up each time for the Snow Queen.

'Rather! Just the ticket.' She was, indeed. He didn't know about the acting stuff but she was a stunner in the looks department and that was all that was required. With make-up and a costume she'd be a knockout. He'd tried to get a word with her after the read-through, but no luck, though he fancied she'd noticed him all right. Caught his eye once. Probably wondering who he was. Well, she'd find out soon enough. Their paths were bound to cross, and then who knew what might happen?

'What a dreary collection of people, Kenny. I wish I'd never agreed to be in their ridiculous play. I can't do the Tuesday rehearsals in any case. We'll be in London. And we'll have people staying at the weekends so Sunday will be impossible too.'

'You can't let them down, Joan. They're counting on you for the star part, to give it some glamour.'

'Then they'll have to find someone else.'

'I doubt if there is anyone else in the village who could do it.'

'Well, they should have thought of that before they started. I imagined it might be some fun, like in a pantomime, but they're taking it all so seriously. I couldn't possibly ask any of our friends to come and see it. They'd be bored out of their minds.'

'They might find it rather charming. Something different. Simple village entertainment.'

'Well, the village will just *simply* have to manage without me. By the way, Kenny, I've asked the Bournes to come next weekend. I think I'll get the Colonel over for dinner on Saturday. He's one of the few civilized people I've met here so far.'

'He may be busy.'

'Busy? In Frog End?'

SEVEN

The Colonel collected the pallet from Naomi first thing in the morning. It was leaning forlornly against the wall beyond her greenhouse and much larger and heavier than he had expected – seven thick planks wide.

Naomi urged him on. 'I'll be glad to get rid of it, Hugh. I want to plant a nice climber there.'

He looked at the wet and dirty wood hammered brutally together which would somehow have to be transformed into a queenly sledge. A tall order, as the Major had remarked. Between them, and with some difficulty, they dragged the unwieldy thing round to Pond Cottage and set it down by the shed.

Naomi moved towards the door. 'I'll help you get it inside.'

He said firmly, 'That's very kind of you, Naomi, but I'll have to do the cutting outside so we may as well leave it here for the moment.'

'How about getting started right now?'

'There's no rush, is there? Christmas is a month away.'

'Marjorie will want it for rehearsals.'

'The cast are still learning their lines.'

'The Snow Queen has hardly got any to speak of. All she has to say is "Come with me, my child, and I will take you to my beautiful palace in the land of ice and snow." And all that sort of stuff. It's a doddle for her.'

'Then there's even more time.'

She went away reluctantly and as soon as she was safely out of the cottage gate he went back to the shed and unlocked it. The irony was that he wouldn't need all the smart new tools he had bought, and which seemed to have somehow got him into this situation in the first place. If Naomi's DIY instructions were to be believed, all that would be required was a saw, a hammer, a chisel and some nails, though, given the rough state of the wood, the sander would certainly come in useful.

He got started. He sawed through the thick bottom struts to narrow the pallet to five planks wide, leaving three spare for the runners. When that was done, he manoeuvred both parts into the shed and propped them against the workbench to dry out. Then he went into the cottage to make himself a cup of tea. He stood drinking it, looking out of the window above the kitchen sink that gave him a view of the garden.

It was already getting dark. In his book, November was the worst month of the year. A grey, depressing time with a long haul ahead before spring. Thank God it would soon be over. He had bought some new daffodil bulbs in October – a pale variety that he had liked rather than the strident yellows – and added them to the others already planted in the rough grass at the end of the garden. They would be something to look forward to. So would Naomi's Three Ships snowdrops that might come into flower by Christmas, if they had survived their peremptory transplant. And Ruth's valiant hellebores would continue to bring cheer. It also occurred to him that bluebells could be just the thing as well for the long grass, if he could find out how to get hold of some.

He had never taken much interest in flowers or gardens before, having spent most of his life without any personal involvement in either, and when he had moved into Pond Cottage he had barely been able to tell a daffodil from a daisy. Thanks to Naomi, he had begun to learn. It had been a slow process but he had reached the stage where he had begun to understand what gardening, even in a very modest, amateur way, was about. It was, he had discovered, not only a source of pleasure but of solace. A reflection of one's inner feelings and thoughts. Show me your garden and I shall tell you what you are. He had read that somewhere and there was probably some truth in it, though he wasn't quite sure what that made him.

The garden at Pond Cottage had been a bramble-choked, nettle-smothered mess when he had arrived. Naomi had encouraged him to clear it and made helpful suggestions, given him spare plants and lent him an excellent gardening book, but she had insisted on him making his own choices. The whole point, she had maintained, was that it should be *his* garden. Mistakes and all. Every gardener made mistakes, apparently, and they could always be rectified; plants moved, new ideas tried out and old ones done away with. And through the garden at Pond Cottage he had somehow regained his faltering grip on life. Found a reason to carry on.

Thursday appeared from the direction of the sitting room and went to sit in front of his food bowl. An early supper was, apparently, required. The Colonel got out a tin of cat food that had NEW RECIPE printed in large letters across the label. Tempting Fish Morsels for Discerning Cats. He forked it into the bowl and stood back. Thursday approached the tempting fish morsels as cautiously as a soldier entering a minefield. He sniffed at them several times before he walked away towards the kitchen door and waited again, ignoring the perfectly good cat flap that had been specially installed for him. The Colonel bowed as he opened the door.

He went into the sitting room to light the fire. It caught quickly, flames leaping and crackling, and he sat down in his wing-back chair and picked up the newspaper. He had just read the front page when the phone rang.

'Hallo, Dad.'

He had braced himself for his daughter-in-law and it was a relief to hear his daughter's voice instead and not be addressed as 'Father'.

'How are you, Alison?'

'Fine, thanks. Busy, as usual. How about you?'

'Fine too.'

She would be phoning from her office high up on the thirty-third floor of a glass building in the City. She was extremely successful in her work and a director of her company. He was very proud of her, but he still wished that she could be happily married as well. He rarely broached the subject and her answer was always that she had never met any man she would want to spend the rest of her life with, or who would want to spend his with her. 'You and Mum are a hard act to follow,' was her usual comment. 'You set the bar pretty high.'

Being left alone as one grew old was not something he could recommend, which was why he feared for her. But he kept his black dog days from both his children. They had their own lives to lead.

'I was thinking of coming down to see you the weekend after next, if that would be OK, Dad?'

'Of course it would. Come on Friday, if you can.'

'I don't think I could get away till Saturday. I've got a late meeting. It's pretty hectic here, as usual.'

'Saturday it is, then. We'll go to the pub for lunch.'

They talked for a while and he had just put down the phone when the front door bell rang. Not Marjorie Cuthbertson, he most sincerely hoped.

'I've found you at last.'

Joan Dryden was wearing the same wolf fur coat that had so impressed, or shocked, the Frog End Players at the village hall read-through. She wore it with the collar turned up and framing her face, her hands dug deep into the pockets, her bucket-sized bag slung over her shoulder. In his opinion, real fur looked far better on its original owner but, in this case, he was almost prepared to make an exception. Almost, but not quite.

He said, 'I'm sorry if you've had trouble doing so.'

'I wanted to phone but I didn't know your surname so I couldn't look you up in the book. All I knew was that you were the Colonel and you lived in a cottage on the village green. I've been to four of them already and the woman in the last one was some funny old maid who wasn't at all helpful. I don't think she wanted to tell me which cottage was yours. I had to ask her very nicely. Can I come in?'

He showed her into the sitting room.

'How cosy! I rather envy you. We positively rattle around in Hassels and it's freezing cold, even with the heating full on.'

He took the heavy coat from her shoulders and laid it over a chair. How many wolves had given their lives for it? Four? Five? Six? It was hard to say.

'Please sit down, Mrs Dryden.'

She took Thursday's place, and Naomi's. Luckily neither was there to mind.

'Do call me Joan. What do I call you?'

'Hugh.'

'I've always liked that name. There's something very attractive about it.'

'Can I offer you a cup of tea?'

'A drink would be much better. Vodka and tonic, if you have it.'

'Ice?'

'And lemon.'

He went away to make her drink, pouring a plain tonic for himself to keep her polite company. He wondered why she had called. 'How are you settling in?'

'Packing cases everywhere still. Kenny says he's too busy to help and my dear daughter won't lift a finger, of course. She just lies around all day doing absolutely nothing.'

He remembered Alison coming down from London to help him with his cases when he had moved into Pond Cottage, making light work of a depressing and sometimes harrowing job. Unwrapping things that belonged to the past: books, ornaments, pictures, vases, lamps, framed photographs that he and Alison had both known well from the time when Laura had been alive and which had gone with them from one soulless army married quarters to the next, transforming them immediately into a home. He had doubted whether the same would happen with Pond Cottage. He had done his best, but Laura's magic touch was missing.

'I'm sorry to hear that.'

'Don't worry, I'm used to it. We've never got on since the day she was born. It's entirely mutual. Clarissa hates me and I can't stand her either. In fact, I wish she'd never been born. Does that shock you, Hugh?'

'No. But it's very sad that you should feel like that. Perhaps things will improve as she grows older.'

'I don't think so.'

'Is she studying?'

'Studying! That's a joke. Clarissa has never studied in her life. Her last school finally got fed up with her and kicked her out, and several others before that one did the same. None of them would keep her. Now she's hanging around, waiting for Kenny to buy her a flat in London. You see, she's cottoned on to the idea that the worse she behaves the sooner he will, just to get rid of her.'

'Surely not.'

'It's true, but I won't bore you with the subject any longer. Actually, I came to ask you to have dinner with us a week on Saturday. We have some old friends, the Bournes, staying over that weekend. I think you'd enjoy meeting them.'

'That's very kind of you but my daughter is coming down from London.'

'Bring her too.'

He said, 'You'll have to excuse us, I'm afraid. Alison and I don't see each other very often.'

'You'd have all the rest of the weekend.'

'It never seems quite enough.'

'Your daughter must be very different from mine.'

'Well, she's a good deal older, for one thing. She's in her late thirties.'

'Married?'

'No.'

'Partner?'

What an inadequate word it was, he thought. Partners were for forming companies, playing bridge or tennis, or dancing with. It had nothing to do with two people sharing their lives. The English language – so rich in words – had failed miserably to come up with anything better.

'No, not that either. I wonder if you realize that the Players rehearse every Sunday afternoon? They'll be expecting you to turn up.'

'So I gather. Actually, Hugh, I've decided that I really can't take part in that tedious play. Mrs Cuthbertson will have to find another Snow Queen.'

'What a shame. You would have been perfect.'

'I don't have much to say or do.'

'But you're the central character. The title and the whole point of the story. And they won't be able to find anyone else who looks nearly as good.'

'That's their problem, not mine.'

He said, 'I'm sure there's no need for you to be at all

the rehearsals. Just the last few, to get the moves right and practise with the sledge.'

'Sledge? What sledge?'

He smiled slowly. 'The one I'm making for you.'

'You're making it?'

'I'm doing my best. I'm afraid it's nothing special. Just some old planks nailed together, but I'll be painting them white to make them look as good as possible. And it's going to have concealed wheels so that you can be pulled across the stage. If you remember from the read-through, the Snow Queen enters and entices the boy, Kai, to go away with her to her ice palace at the North Pole. It should be a proper horse-drawn sleigh, of course, complete with jingle bells, but unfortunately the Players can't run to that, and nor can the village hall stage, so it will have to be the home-made sledge.'

She stared at him. 'Is this meant to be funny, Hugh?'

'Not at all. It's very serious.' He smiled at her again. 'You'll be perfect in the part, and I promise to do my best with the sledge.'

Freda Butler adjusted the U-boat commander's binoculars to improve her view of the Colonel's cottage on the other side of the green. It was surprising how well she could see with them even when it was dark. No doubt, the captain would have used them at night, too, searching for his prey. Convoy ships were blacked out, she knew, but their silhouettes would still have been visible in certain conditions, especially in full moonlight. Unlike the U-boat commander, she had the advantage of the Colonel's sitting-room lamp as an aiming point. Fortunately, he had not yet drawn the curtains.

Sometime earlier, Mrs Dryden had parked her car outside Lupin Cottage and knocked at her door – unnecessarily loudly. She had seemed very put-out when Miss Butler had opened it, having concealed the binoculars.

'Oh! I was looking for the Colonel.'

She had been wearing that dreadful fur coat – real fur – that she had worn for the village hall read-through. Miss Butler found it very upsetting to think of the poor animals who had died to provide it. Wolves, she thought, and several of them. They might be savage on occasion, but they were still God's creatures and entitled to live out their lives. In fact, she had recently read a very interesting article in a newspaper that had said that wolves were good for the environment because they preyed on deer that would otherwise strip young trees bare if left to browse unthreatened. Thanks to wolves keeping the deer numbers down, forests and plants flourished, providing a habitat for birds and all kinds of species.

She had said, very politely, 'I'm afraid the Colonel doesn't live here.'

'Well, can you tell me where he does?'

The tone was impatient but Miss Butler had held her ground. After all, an Englishman's home was his castle – not to be disclosed to all and sundry.

'I don't think we've met.'

'I'm Joan Dryden. My husband and I have moved into Hassels recently. I'd like to return the Colonel's call on us – if someone will kindly tell me where he lives.'

Of course, Miss Butler already knew perfectly well who the woman was – the whole village knew – and she also happened to be familiar with her other name, Joan Lowe. She had once been famous for modelling clothes and her name and photograph had often appeared in the popular press – though that had been some years ago. If Miss Butler remembered correctly – and she usually did – there had been a big scandal when she had run off with Mr Dryden while he was actually married to someone else. Today, of course, nobody would be in the least shocked. It happened all the time. She seemed to remember, too, that his first wife had tragically committed suicide after he had left her. There had been quite a bit about it in the newspapers.

'I'm not sure if he's at home.'

'I can find that out for myself.'

She had stuck to her guns. 'He may be working in his shed, in which case he won't wish to be disturbed.'

'I don't think he'll mind if it's me, do you?'

It had been a valiant but vain attempt to spare the Colonel. In the end, she had been obliged to point out Pond Cottage, across the green, where the lamp was glowing in the sitting-room window.

What a dreadful woman! As she had suspected, Joan Dryden had a lot in common with the late Lady Swynford. She found herself disliking her quite as much.

It was almost an hour now since she had watched Mrs Dryden drive away round the green to Pond Cottage. She had tracked her up the path to the front door, seen the Colonel open it and Mrs Dryden go inside, then watched them moving around the sitting room.

And she was still there.

'You're early, Naomi.'

'I've come to protect you.'

'From what?'

'From the likes of Joan Dryden. I thought she'd never leave, Hugh.'

'I assure you, protection is not required. How did you know she was here, anyway?'

'I looked out of my window and saw that flashy car of hers parked outside your gate.'

Child's play for the Frog End KGB, he thought. They would know to the minute what time his visitor had arrived and exactly what time she had left. The 'funny old maid' mentioned by Joan Dryden as her fourth port of call round the green would have been Freda Butler, who was doubtless still on conning-tower duty from her sitting-room window.

'Well, come in and have a drink.'

'Jolly good idea!'

Thursday, who had just settled himself comfortably in his fireside place on the sofa, was re-parked at the other end while the Colonel drew the curtains, thwarting Miss Butler, put on another log and poured the drinks.

'Good health, Naomi.'

'Cheers, Hugh. What did she want?'

'To invite me to dinner. She has some friends visiting soon for the weekend.'

'Are you going?'

'No. Alison is coming down.'

'That's nice for you. And a good excuse.'

He said drily, 'She didn't seem to think so.'

'I don't suppose people often refuse her.'

'Probably not.'

'Well, I hope she's going to turn up for the rehearsal on Sunday afternoon.'

'She's actually decided to opt out completely.'

'Oh, Hugh, that would be disastrous! We'll be left with Monica Pudsey.'

'I may have managed to persuade her to stay.'

'How?'

'For one thing, I told her I didn't think there was any need to attend every single rehearsal.'

'There isn't. She's only on a few times and hardly says anything. I'll have a word with Marjorie and she'll sort it out.'

'I also told her about the sledge that I was making especially for her to be pulled around on.'

'What did she say?'

'She thought it sounded rather amusing.'

'Amusing?'

'Well, difficult to take seriously.'

'I hope Marjorie doesn't get to hear that.'

'I assured her that it was far from a joke. Especially for me.'

'How are you getting on with it, by the way?'

'I've made a start.'

'Good. Can I see it?'

He said kindly but firmly, 'No, Naomi. You may not.'

EIGHT

Alison arrived on Saturday morning. The Colonel hadn't seen his daughter for several months and, as always, it was a pleasure. He kissed her cheek and she smiled up at him.

'You're looking well, Dad.'

'So are you.'

But he thought that she looked tired.

'It's mostly make-up, Dad. I'm about to have a breakdown from overworking.'

'Lucky you're taking a holiday soon.'

'Can't wait. But I'm sorry I won't be spending Christmas with you, like last year.'

'I think you'll find Zermatt has rather more to offer than Frog End.'

'You know, I used to think it was deadly here but I've changed my mind, now that I've got to know it better. And it seems to suit you, Dad.'

'It does.'

'But Marcus says you're going to them for Christmas.'

'That's the general idea.'

'Will you survive Susan?'

Alison had never made any secret to him of her poor opinion of her sister-in-law. He regretted it as much as his own inability to feel closer to his son's wife.

He said, 'It's very good of them to ask me.'

'Well, don't let her persuade you to go and live near them. You'd hate it.'

'I won't.'

'I see Thursday's still condescending to stay.'

Alison was a cat person, like Marjorie Cuthbertson, otherwise Thursday would never have come into the sitting room. He walked past her and jumped up on to the sofa where he allowed her to pat his head before he settled down, paws folded

beneath his chin, blinking his eyes slowly, prepared to listen
to their conversation.

'Yes, I'm in favour at the moment.'

'Well, he knows he's on to a good thing, Dad. Cats aren't
fools.'

They walked over to the Dog and Duck for lunch. It was
rather a shame that the pub had been done up since the time
he had visited it many years ago when he and Laura had been
touring in Dorset. In those days there had been an old flag-
stone floor, heavy wooden settles, draught beer, cheese and
pickle sandwiches and Smiths crisps. Now the flagstones had
disappeared under a patterned carpet, the benches had been
replaced by modern chairs, the beer came out of a keg and
a new extension had been built on the back of the pub where
full meals were served. Still, one had to move with the times.
Or rather, pubs did, if they wanted to keep in business.

The Major was in his usual place at the bar, holding forth
to anyone who would listen about the state of the country
which was, as usual, going to the dogs.

'They let all these damned foreigners in. Can't speak a word
of English, breed like rabbits, given free housing, handouts
and all the rest of it and never a word of thanks. They ought
to send them back where they came from.'

They slid past unnoticed.

'I've got some news for you, Dad,' Alison said when they
were settled at a table. 'I've met someone.'

'Oh? That sounds very interesting.'

'He's rather special, actually. Twelve years older than me.
Something pretty successful in the City. The only snag is that
he's married.'

'That is quite a snag.'

'He and his wife have been growing apart for years – each
doing their own thing, if you follow me.'

'I think I do. Are there any children?'

'One daughter. She's twenty-two. Flown the nest into her
own flat, complete with partner.'

That unsatisfactory word again.

He said, 'Are you in love with him?'

'I'm not sure, to be honest. I like him a lot. We speak the

same language. Enjoy the same sort of things. Get on well together. It might work. We'll see. I haven't known him that long.'

'Does he still live with his wife?'

'No, he's moved out into a rather nice penthouse right on the river. The north side. Lady Bracknell would approve no end. He wants me to move in there too.'

'How about the shirts that you've always sworn you'll never iron?'

'He gets them done by a laundry.'

'Will you move in?'

'I haven't decided. It would be quite a step. I'm rather used to being on my own.'

She had the advantage of him, he realized. It was something he had yet to grow used to.

'Well, keep me posted, won't you?'

'I promise.' She smiled wryly. 'I can see you don't approve, Dad. It's written all over your face.'

It wasn't what he and Laura had always hoped for her. Of course it wasn't. Laura, he knew, had had high hopes of a white wedding, a handsome young bridegroom, of them living happily ever after together as husband and wife in the very old-fashioned way. No baggage or complications or partners. Alison hadn't mentioned marriage and he doubted if that was in her mind, or that of the man in question. But at least she had found someone she liked a lot, who spoke the same language and enjoyed the same sort of things. It could be a lot better than nobody at all.

'I don't disapprove,' he said. 'I just don't want you to be hurt or made unhappy.'

'I won't be. If things don't work out I'll just walk away.'

But he knew it wouldn't be that simple. It rarely was.

They went to church on Sunday morning, as he usually did out of sheer habit. The new young vicar had recruited him some time ago as a sidesman. It involved simple jobs like putting out the candlesticks, giving out hymn books and so on. His turn came on the second Sunday of every other month, which was hardly arduous and difficult to refuse. Unfortunately, the vicar also thought that he had a good speaking voice – the sort, he'd said, that people would find easy to listen to – and he had also asked if he would read the lesson occasionally. This was rather a different matter since it meant him standing up and reading words aloud that he didn't believe in. He had reasoned, though, that it was probably no more dishonest than singing hymns with words that he didn't believe in either, automatically reciting prayers known by heart since childhood or responding, where required, with dutiful amens.

He had read the instructions given in the Book of Common Prayer about lesson reading and they were clear and uncom-promising. *It must be read distinctly with an audible voice . . . he that readeth so standing and turning himself, as he may best be heard of all such as are present.* This Sunday happened to be Advent Sunday, and it was his turn to read the second lesson, taken from the New Testament.

They sat halfway down the nave at the end of one of the old pews that the same well-meaning vicar had planned to do away with to provide an open space for village activities. The public meeting held to discuss his controversial proposal had resulted in the total rejection of any such thing. Similarly, the idea of using a new, modern form of service and the congre-gation making kindly signs of peace to each other had been strangled at birth. The Colonel had not expressed any opinion. He himself had been a non-believer since his wife's suffering and death but he could understand that the old rituals and words were a comfort to many people and why they fought to keep them.

At the very last moment before the service began the Drydens arrived, rather as the late Lady Swynford of the Manor used to do. Joan Dryden was wearing her wolf coat and with a hat to match. Another wolf sacrificed, or at least, part of one. Heads swivelled as she made straight for the front pew, followed by her husband and another couple who must be the weekend guests she had mentioned, dressed in faultless country tweeds. The Colonel wondered if they ever went to church in London or whether it was all part of the Marie Antoinette game. It was no surprise that the teenage daughter was absent.

They responded obediently to all the prayers, confessed their sins humbly on their knees, recited the Lord's Prayer loudly – being the one that everyone knew, mumbled their way through Psalm 95, and sang the Advent hymn 'Lo! He Comes With Clouds Descending'. The first lesson, taken from Isaiah, was read by a village worthy and soon it was the Colonel's turn to read from Luke 1, verses 5–20. He followed the prayer book instructions to the letter.

'"There was in the days of Herod, the king of Judea, a certain priest name Zacharias . . ."'

By verse eleven, he could tell that he'd got them hooked. They were all listening.

'"And there appeared unto him an angel of the Lord standing on the right side of the altar of incense . . ."'

Even the Major was paying attention.

'"Fear not, Zacharias: for thy prayer is heard; and thy wife Elisabeth shall bear thee a son, and thou shalt call his name John . . . I am Gabriel, that stand in the presence of God; and am sent to speak unto thee these glad tidings."'

As he passed the front pew, returning to his seat, Joan Dryden mimed applause.

Another hymn: 'Thy kingdom come! On bended knee the passing ages pray.' There was no need to look down at his hymn book – the Colonel knew all the words.

He listened to the earnest young vicar delivering a long sermon on repentance and the forgiveness of sins that had the Major pulling out his pocket watch, shaking it and holding it to his ear.

At the end of the service, Joan and her wolves barred their way out of the church door. He introduced Alison.

'I insist that you join us at Hassels for a pre-lunch drink, Hugh. And I won't take no for an answer.'

He would have declined, whether she would take it or not, but he could tell that Alison was intrigued.

'That's kind of you, Joan.'

She lowered her voice. 'It isn't kindness, Hugh. You'll be doing me a favour. I'd forgotten how boring the Bournes can be. Don't let me down, for heaven's sake.'

He watched her rejoin the boring friends.

Alison said, 'Who on earth was that, Dad?'

'A resident celebrity. She's married to Kenneth Dryden

who's something on TV and they've just bought a house here.
She used to be Joan Lowe.'

'I've heard of her, and him. He did rather good travel documentaries, didn't he? And she was a supermodel, years ago.
She still looks pretty good.'

'Yes, she does.'

'I seem to remember they were both married to someone
else and there was a huge scandal when they went off together.
Of course, it was different in the old days.'

It might be taken more lightly today, he thought, but the
collateral damage was probably much the same.

At Hassels, the hall had been cleared of packing cases and
the drawing room was transformed. He wondered how it had
been achieved.

Joan Dryden said, 'I've found a marvellous woman in the
village to help with things. An absolute treasure.'

'That's good.'

'Do you like the wall colour?'

'Very much.'

'I chose Ashes in the end. My tame painter rushed down
from London especially to do it, bless him. What do you think
of the curtains?'

'Very beautiful.'

'I bought them from an old friend of mine who deals in
antique ones. Hideously expensive, of course, but they make
most new curtains look cheap and nasty. I thought they rather
suited the house.'

'They do indeed.'

'Kenny, tell Clarissa to come down and be sociable for once.'

The daughter appeared, scowling. Far better to have left her
upstairs, the Colonel thought. He remembered Joan's remark:
'Clarissa hates me and I can't stand her either.' A wretched
situation, if it was really true.

Kenneth Dryden said to him, aside, 'Clarissa would be much
happier in London but Joan and I are afraid of what she'd get
up to there without us.'

The Colonel went over to the girl to attempt a conversation
but she answered him in sullen monosyllables. She was nice
looking beneath the tangle of hair, though not in the same

league as her mother. Perhaps that was the problem? Jealousy? Rivalry? On both sides? Were difficult children made or were they born like that? he wondered. There was no easy answer. After a moment, she muttered some excuse and left the room.

Her father said to him, 'I'm afraid she's somewhat lacking in social graces.'

Her mother intervened. 'Somewhat, Kenny? Totally, you mean. Make her come back and apologise.'

'There's no point in that, Joan.'

'So she gets away with it every time. Well, I apologise for her, Hugh. Clarissa is an embarrassing disgrace. You're very lucky to have such a charming daughter of your own.'

He knew that he was. Neither Alison nor Marcus had ever been any trouble or in any way difficult. His only worry, always shared by Laura, was for their children's personal happiness. His son's marriage had gone through a distinctly rocky patch when he'd lost his job, and the married man could mean heartbreak for Alison.

He changed the subject. 'Your sledge is coming along, Joan. Some way to go, but I hope you'll be pleased with it when it's finished.'

'I'd like to see what I'm letting myself in for.'

'Not just yet.'

He had separated out the three leftover planks and sawn across their ends at an angle. Then he had nailed them to the underneath of the platform, one at each side and one in the middle, the angled ends protruding at the front to form runners. It was rudimentary, to say the least, and certainly not ready for the Snow Queen's critical inspection.

'How did you know I was still going to play the part, anyway, Hugh?'

'News travels fast in Frog End.'

'That old battleaxe came to see me about the rehearsals, you know. I told her that I can't do Tuesdays because we'll be in London and I couldn't possibly do every Sunday. It's out of the question. She climbed down after that. They seem rather keen to have me.'

'I'm sure they are.'

*   *   *

Later, on their way back to Pond Cottage, Alison said, 'What was all that about a sledge, Dad?'

'I'm making her one.'

'What on earth for? I can't see her going tobogganing.'

'She's playing the Snow Queen in the Frog End Players' Christmas entertainment. The sledge is meant to be a magical sleigh, though it falls rather short. They usually do a panto-mime but this year it's the Hans Christian Andersen story.'

'I remember reading it years ago. The Snow Queen is extremely beautiful but has a heart of ice, hasn't she?' Alison laughed. 'She'll be perfect.'

NINE

The Major had finished reading his Sunday paper and fallen into a comfortable doze by the time his wife returned from the Frog End Players' rehearsal. He was awoken by the crash of the front door closing and footsteps thudding down the hall, and when she flung open the sitting-room door he could tell by her face that things had not gone at all well.

Apart from the Gerda character, apparently, nobody knew their lines. The boy, Kai, had read most of his and not very well either. The kindly old grandmother had been inaudible, the dastardly robbers out of control and the dancing snowflakes more like elephants. As for the raven, who was meant to be an important character in the story, hopping about boldly, he'd acted more like a pathetic sparrow. If the cast didn't pull their socks up the play would turn out to be a disaster.

'Sorry to hear that,' the Major said. 'You know, old Toby might be just the job for the raven. He was rather cut up to be left out of things this year.'

'Mr Jugge is not taking part in this entertainment, Roger. I thought I'd made that very clear.'

'Just a suggestion, dear. Just a suggestion.'

'And a very poor one. Of course, it didn't help that Mrs Dryden wasn't present. I had to stand in for her, as well as direct. I agreed to her missing the next two Sunday rehearsals but after that she really must be there. Before we know where we are Christmas will be upon us.'

It was not a prospect that cheered the Major. When they'd been posted abroad, Christmases had always been jolly good fun. Army chaps knew how to enjoy themselves. Full of *joie de vivre* and all that. But Christmases hadn't been quite the same since he and Marjorie had come back home and retired to Frog End. And this Snow Queen thing wasn't going to help, by the sound of it. Not much *joie* there.

At first, he'd rather fancied his chances with Joan Dryden,

but whenever their paths had crossed she'd ignored him completely. Cut him dead, in fact. Well, he could take a hint. She was a pretty cold fish, anyway. There were plenty of warmer ones in the sea. Maybe not in Frog End, but around and about. Never say die. That was his motto. *Nil desperandum.* Though lately, he'd begun to despair a bit, to wonder if life had passed him by. He wasn't getting any younger, that was for sure. *Tempus fugit*, and all that. A depressing thought, if ever there was one.

He glanced hopefully at his late mother-in-law's clock on the mantelpiece. Slow again! Inspiration struck.

'You could do with a pick-me-up, old girl.' So could he, come to that. 'I'll get you one.'

He stood up smartly.

'Sit down, Roger. It's only twenty past five.'

'That damned clock's always slow.'

'Mother's clock keeps perfect time. It's you that doesn't.'

He sat down again and retired behind his newspaper, looking hurt and disinclined to sympathise any more. 'Well, I wouldn't worry too much. I dare say it will all be all right on the night.'

The Colonel was fairly satisfied with progress on the sledge.

He had bought some more wood and constructed arms at each side of the pallet platform for the Snow Queen. It would be unthinkable for her to fall off mid-stage. That done, he spent a long time sanding all the wood to a smooth finish. Equally unthinkable for her to get splinters anywhere.

The next problem was the wheels. He took Naomi's advice and called on Steph, formerly Steve, at the local garage.

He found him under a car bonnet and put the problem to him.

'I'll think of something, Colonel. Leave it to me.'

An arrow-pierced heart with the letters S and N had been added to the multiple tattoos on Steph's right arm, he noticed. Space had somehow been found for it among the writhing serpents.

'That's very good of you, Steph.'

'No problem. I like a challenge.'

He drove on into Dorchester to do some shopping in the

supermarket where several shelves were devoted to cat food varied enough to appeal to the most picky consumer – even Thursday. He was trying to decide between Nine Lives Beef in Tomato Sauce and Munchies Grilled Fish Medley when another customer kindly offered advice.

'I'd go for the Munchies if I were you, Colonel. It's a very good brand.'

He smiled and thanked the woman, whoever she was. She evidently knew him, and her face was vaguely familiar, but he couldn't remember where they had met. Recognizing people out of context and in different clothing was sometimes difficult. He had once puzzled for days over the strange young man who had hailed him cheerily in a town street before he had realized that it was the Frog End postman who came daily to his cottage door.

The woman said, 'Cats can be very choosy eaters, can't they?'

'They can, indeed.'

'And you can't make them do things they don't want to do.'

'That's also very true.'

'The trouble is people tend to see their cats as being like a less demanding dog but, of course, they're quite different. A cat is halfway between domestic and wild and they have their own particular way of doing things. Owners expect to receive the same amount of devotion shown by dogs, but cats have other things on their minds.'

Thursday would have been entirely on her side.

'You just have the one?'

'Oh, yes. That's another mistake people often make. They imagine that cats need the company of other cats, so they get another one, or even more, thinking it's a nice idea. But cats aren't necessarily very good with other cats. They need their own space and it's usually very well-defined.'

He smiled, thinking of the fire end of the sofa. 'I've noticed that.'

They exchanged cat talk pleasantly for a moment before moving on. He was halfway home before he remembered who she was. Naomi had introduced her at *The Snow Queen* read-through in the village hall. She was the one who did the make-up for the Frog End Players, who could make anyone look good. Ironically, she was also the one who never wore any make-up herself and who Naomi had rather accurately described as fading into the background. Her name was Thora Jay, if he remembered correctly.

'Dad, can I ask you something?'

Kenneth Dryden sighed. The chat show had been even more hellish than usual, the guest line-up near insupportable: a cocky young chef making some revolting dish that he was expected to sample with lip-smacking relish, an aged actor who was losing his marbles as fast as his hair, a long-forgotten comedian who was no longer remotely funny and a woman who solemnly swore she had been abducted by aliens who had landed in her back garden from outer space. All he wanted now was to be left in peace with his stiff drink.

'What is it, Clarissa?'

'Why can't I have a flat, Dad? No one else I know still lives with their parents. It's pathetic.'

She was using the whining voice that he hated and looking her sulkiest. He wanted to smack her face. Perhaps he should have done so long ago? He'd made a rod for his own back by spoiling her rotten.

'We've already discussed this and I've told you why. In the first place you're too young, and in the second, I can't afford it.'

'You give Mum everything she wants.'

'Your mother is entitled to every care and consideration. And I'm not sure that you are, Clarissa, seeing how badly you behave.'

'I'll just leave, then. Go away for ever. Mum'd be thrilled. She can't wait to get rid of me.'

He knew it was true. Joan had told him so many times.

'And where exactly would you go?'

'I'd find somewhere. Lots of my friends have flats. They have trusts and things.'

'Unfortunately, you don't. So, what exactly would you live on?'

'I'd get a job.'

'As what? You have no qualifications whatsoever. You've never done a day's work in your life and, on present showing,

I doubt you're capable of such a thing.'

'You could give me an allowance.'

'No, I couldn't, Clarissa. You have to learn to behave a great deal better: to show us some manners, some respect. Then perhaps your mother and I will see what we can do.'

'Mum won't do anything for me. She hates me. Don't you realize that? And I loathe her. I wish she was dead!'

'Don't be absurd. You don't mean that.'

'Oh, yes, I do. And if you make me go on living with her I'll find a way to kill her. So you'd better do something about it.'

The door slammed hard behind his daughter, leaving Kenneth Dryden alone but far from in peace.

TEN

Within a week, Steph called by Pond Cottage.
'I found some wheels in a skip that might do the trick, Colonel. Look like they probably belonged to one of those old-fashioned kiddies' pushchairs. Nice and solid. They'll need new axles fitted so I've brought the pickup to take your sledge to the workshop and do the job there.'

'That's very good of you, Steph.'

'Always glad to lend a hand. When people treat me right, I do the same.'

The Colonel led the way to the shed. The pallet sledge was propped on its side against the workbench. Steph bent to take a closer, professional look. If he saw faults in its amateur construction, he was too polite to say so.

'I reckon we can make something of her all right, Colonel. She's good and strong, that's for sure. All we've got to do is get her rolling.'

In spite of its lumpish looks, the sledge was, apparently, feminine, like cars and ships.

They carried her out to the pickup and loaded her into the back.

The Colonel had no doubt that they were being watched by many pairs of curious eyes, including those of Miss Butler, which would be glued to her Zeiss binoculars at the front window of Lupin Cottage across the green.

Freda Butler was quite unable to make out what exactly it was that the Colonel and Steve from the garage were heaving into the truck. She twiddled the knob on the binoculars in vain, for it didn't make the mysterious object any more identifiable. Something wooden and heavy, and which, presumably, the Colonel had made in his shed, though she had always understood that he usually worked on much smaller things – model tanks and planes and so on. There was no reason why he

should have told her anything about it, of course, but it was
odd that she had not heard something through the village
grapevine. And why was Steve involved? Having no car herself,
relying instead on the somewhat unreliable local bus service,
she rarely came across him and knew very little about him.
Someone had said that he now called himself Steph, which
was even stranger.

She kept the binoculars trained on the pickup and its
mysterious cargo as Steve, or Steph, drove off. The Colonel
stood outside his cottage gate for a moment, watching it go,
and then went back inside.

It was tempting to invent some excuse to call on him but
none came to her mind. Still, it should be a simple matter to
find out what the thing was. Someone in the village was bound
to know.

Rehearsals of *The Snow Queen* proceeded under the draconian
direction of Mrs Cuthbertson. The Colonel attended one of
them, partly out of a misplaced sense of duty and partly out
of curiosity.

The play was slowly coming together. Lines had been
learned, though Naomi, who was prompter again this year,
still had plenty to do, since they were frequently forgotten
again. And the director herself was hampered by having to
stand in for Joan Dryden, who had only turned up for one
Sunday rehearsal so far. The Colonel watched Mrs Cuthbertson
striding around the village hall stage, script in hand, barking
out the Snow Queen's seductive lines.

'Come with me, my child, and I will take you to my beautiful palace in the land of ice and snow.'

The boy, Kai, to whom these words were addressed,
unwisely sniggered.

Thora Jay came to stand beside the Colonel. 'Shouldn't Mrs
Dryden be here?'

He said drily, 'I don't think it's in her contract.'

'I was hoping to get some ideas for her make-up.'

'What do you have in mind?'

'Something icy. Very Snow Queen.'

Theatrical make-up, he realized, must require special skills.

If you were good at it, you could make people look completely unlike their normal selves. Change faces beyond recognition, alter features, put on false noses and chins and ears, beards and moustaches, fit wigs or turn people bald, add wrinkles and lines or smooth them away – whatever was required.

'Did you work for the stage?'

'Not always. I was freelance – stage, films, television – which made life interesting. Always new challenges.'

He was curious. 'How did you start?'

'I joined a provincial repertory company, hoping to do some acting, but instead I found myself helping with the make-up. I enjoyed it, so I did a specialist course in London, learning all the tricks of the trade, and went on from there.'

'Are there many tricks?'

'Oh, yes. And it's all changed since the old days of heavy greasepaint and pasted-on wigs. I'd have to learn a lot of new techniques. I spent some time with the Royal Shakespeare Company before I retired. Lighting is key now. Modern lighting can completely alter the look of an actor without the need for a lot of make-up. Side lighting can fill out a thin face and make it look younger, for instance; overhead lights can age people dramatically.'

He thought of the village hall's ancient and erratic spotlights, inclined to produce either a watery flicker or a blinding beam.

'You must find our lighting a bit of a challenge.'

'I've been having a word with Bob Fox, who's in charge. I think we can work out something together.'

There was more to Mrs Jay than met the eye, the Colonel decided. It would be interesting to see what she made of the Snow Queen.

The Major heard the slam of the front door and the *thud, thud, thud* of his wife's footsteps approaching the sitting room. His mother-in-law's clock had chimed six more than half an hour ago, so there was no need for him to feel any guilt about the glass already in his hand. It was all above board. All tickety-boo. He could look the old girl squarely in the face when she came in.

'How did the rehearsal go, dear?'

When she sat down on the sofa he saw the glint of battle in her eye that he had come to know so well over the years.

'Mrs Dryden failed to turn up, yet again. So I went round to Hassels afterwards.'

'Was she at home?'

'She was indeed. There were people staying for the weekend but I didn't let that stop me. I told her straight out that I had decided to get someone else for the part since it was quite impossible for me to continue standing-in for her and also direct the play to the required level of competence.'

You had to admire Marjorie at times, he admitted to himself. Never afraid of speaking her mind and going for the jugular. Right up there with Boadicea.

'What did she say?'

'She said it was fine by her – that she'd never wanted to play the part in the first place. I was just going to walk out of the room but then the weekend people started telling her that she ought to do it and how wonderful she'd be. They all wanted to see her as the Snow Queen, including Mr Dryden. He kept trying to coax her into it, just like last time. I don't know why he bothers. She's not worth it.'

'Well, what happened?'

'She said she'd try to come to the next Sunday rehearsal, though she couldn't promise it. And I told her that if she didn't turn up I'd cast someone else.'

Fighting talk, the Major thought. That's the spirit!

'But who would you get?'

'Mrs Pudsey.'

'*Mrs Pudsey.*'

'Don't stare at me like that, Roger. She'd have to do. There's nobody else. And I dare say Mrs Jay could make her look better with a lot of make-up.'

'She'd need a shovel.'

'I expect you to be positive about this, Roger.'

The Major drained his glass positively. 'You look as though you could do with a sherry, dear. I'll get it for you.'

'Just a small one, then.'

He took his own glass over to the cabinet and 'Drink to Me

Only With Thine Eyes' started up as he opened the lid. With his back turned to the old girl, it was a simple manoeuvre to pour out the Bristol Cream and replenish his whisky as well – a lightning sleight of hand that he had practised a great many times. Sometimes he thought he would have made rather a good conjuror.

'How's the sledge coming along, Hugh?'

'Progress is being made, Naomi.'

'That's good, because Marjorie wants it for a try-out at the next rehearsal on Sunday. Apparently our Snow Queen is deigning to put in an appearance. Marjorie's going to ring you about it and she'll want to know the state of play. You have been warned.'

The interesting thing, the Colonel thought, is that the whole village seemed to be in the dark about the sledge. Steph must have kept it well out of sight and said nothing. He smiled to himself. Quite an achievement.

'Have you painted it yet?'

'No, not yet.'

'Time marches on.'

'I'm well aware of that at my age. And Mrs Bentley has already pointed it out to me.'

'She would.'

'Yes, she would.'

'When I was up in the attic the other day I came across something that might work rather well with the sledge – if it ever gets finished.'

'What exactly?'

'Guess.'

There was no point in attempting such a thing. Naomi's attic harboured all manner of bizarre relics from the past.

'Perhaps you could bring whatever it is round next time?'

'I might – if you show me the sledge.'

'It's not here.'

'Oh?'

'Some adjustments are being made.'

'You mean Steph's doing the wheels? No need to be so secretive, Hugh. You're like an old dog with a buried bone.'

'I feel like it sometimes.'

'We're curious. Will it work or won't it? It's a focal point. The Snow Queen and Marjorie Cuthbertson will be expecting great things of you. So will we all.'

'I'll try not to disappoint you.'

When Marjorie Cuthbertson rang later, she left him in no doubt of what she was expecting. 'I trust the sledge will be ready for the rehearsal on Sunday, Colonel?'

'I'll do my best.'

'We must have it. Mrs Dryden is attending, for once, and we have to take full advantage of the chance to practise with the sledge. It's a very dramatic moment in the play when the Snow Queen lures the boy away to her ice palace. We need to iron out any possible problems.'

He could think of a few. With wheels but without brakes, the sledge might be hard to steer or stop. It might crash into the scenery or even go clean over the edge of the stage into the audience below. Mrs Cuthbertson was perfectly right. Practising was more than a sound idea; it was essential.

The next morning Steph arrived in the pick-up with the sledge fitted with its pushchair wheels. They tried it out on the terrace at the back of the cottage, pulling on the rope. It rolled smoothly across the flagstones, changing direction obediently.

Steph was pleased. 'She shouldn't give any trouble, Colonel.'

He was referring, of course, to the sledge rather than the Snow Queen. In the Colonel's opinion, either or both could give plenty of trouble. Within the cramped confines of the village hall stage things might not go so well as out on the terrace.

They carried the sledge into the shed, ready for the Colonel to paint. It took him three days – priming and undercoating with three top coats on all surfaces before he was satisfied. But no amount of glossy white paint could disguise the sledge's humble pallet origins. Improvisation, as Naomi had said, was the name of the game with the Frog End Players when it came to scenery and props, but this was hardly a conveyance fit for a queen. Something more was needed.

He had gone back into the cottage when there was a loud

knock at the front door. Mrs Cuthbertson come to inspect the sledge? Heaven forbid! He opened it to a polar bear standing upright before him, six feet tall, fangs bared.

'It's only me,' Naomi said from somewhere behind the bear's head. She was holding the bear up by its huge front paws and waggled them at him, the fearsome claws rattling. 'Can we come in?'

In the sitting room she spread the bear out in front of the fireplace, arranging the glass-eyed head and the four legs in place. Thursday watched intently from the sofa.

'What do you think, Hugh?'

'Magnificent. But sad to see.'

'I agree. A great uncle of mine shot it on a trip to the Arctic Circle. He was always shooting things. Lions, tigers, leopards, elephants . . . anything that moved. He had an umbrella stand made from an elephant's foot but I wouldn't have it in the house. I remembered this old chap when we were talking about your sledge the other day. He's been up in the attic for years and gone a bit yellow but he still looks pretty good.'

The polar bear easily surpassed any attic trophy previously brought to light by Naomi – the Cossack wolf hat paling into insignificance. Even so, he couldn't quite fathom the bear's role.

'What exactly am I supposed to do with him?'

'Put him on the sledge, of course. The Snow Queen can sit on him. After all, polar bears come from the North Pole and so does she. Marjorie couldn't ask for anything more suitable.'

He smiled. 'That's true.'

'So, now can I see the sledge?'

'The paint's not dry.'

'I won't touch it.'

'It's out in the shed.'

'I'll stay outside and look at it through the doorway.'

He gave way in the end. It was only fair. He even allowed her inside the shed, turning on the lights and standing back to give her space to view. 'Well, what do you think?'

'I think it looks jolly good, Hugh. You've done an excellent job. But my polar bear will provide the finishing touch. The *coup de théâtre*.'

He had to agree. 'We could try it out on Sunday, if that's all right with you.'

'Yes, let's. I'll help you.' Naomi was looking round the shed. 'I must say this is a jolly nice hideaway, now you've got electricity. No wonder you spend so much time in here.'

'I don't hide away, Naomi.'

'Yes, you do. What are you going to work on next?'

Fortunately, the heirloom rocking horse plans and parts had been stored out of sight. It would be fatal to give Naomi any hint of their existence. Now that she had put her foot not only in the door but through it, she would be counting on doing so again.

'I haven't decided yet,' he said, taking her arm firmly. 'Let's go and have a drink.'

ELEVEN

The sledge made a grand entrance into the village hall where the Frog End Players had gathered for the Sunday rehearsal. Steph had driven it over in the pickup truck and he and the Colonel had wheeled it to the door where Naomi had arranged the skin artfully, head uplifted in a snarl at the front, four paws hanging over the sides, so that the bear appeared to be padding along. As they went in, heads turned and silence fell. Even Marjorie Cuthbertson lost her tongue – temporarily.

'I must say, Colonel, that you've done an extraordinary job. I hadn't expected anything quite so . . . dramatic! Wherever did you get that animal?'

The Players crowded round, stroking the bear. The boy who played Kai climbed on board at once and Steph took him for a spin round the hall. He had completed a circuit when Joan Dryden made her usual late entrance, dressed, as before, by the wolves.

It was quite a sight, the Colonel thought later as they practised up on the stage, with the Snow Queen reclining regally on the sledge, grey wolf upon white polar bear, and Kai crouched in front with his hand on the bear's head. Thanks to Steph's skilful handling of the wheels and ropes, the sledge performed without a hitch.

When the rehearsal proper began, Naomi went off to prompt from the wings and the Colonel sat at the back of the hall, watching.

Things had moved on considerably since the first ragged read-through. The evil sorcerer, owner of the magic mirror that had fallen to earth and shattered into trillions of evil splinters, had toned down his manic cackle, and the girl, Gerda, was word-perfect. The boy, Kai, needed constant prompting from Naomi, but he was trying hard. The kindly old grandmother braved many interruptions from the director's chair.

'I can hardly hear a word you're saying, Mrs Simcocks. You must speak louder or they'll never hear you at the back. Could you hear her, Colonel?'

'Not entirely.'

'Not at all, I should imagine. The grandmother is a key part of the story. If the audience can't hear her, they won't know what's going on.'

The Colonel wasn't too sure himself, but the story seemed the sort of thing that young children would enjoy: the kindly old grandmother's garden where Gerda and Kai played happily together in summer, winter coming when everything would change to snow and bitter cold, the boy's heart and eyes struck by splinters from the sorcerer's broken mirror so that he became cruel to Gerda and the grandmother. Children seldom seemed upset by even the most horrific fairy tales. This one was comparatively tame by comparison.

When Kai went out to play in the snow with other boys, the Colonel waited with interest for the Snow Queen to arrive on the polar bear sledge and carry him off.

She did not disappoint. Joan Dryden not only looked the part, she had learned it. Her few lines were delivered in glacial tones that, unlike the kindly old grandmother's, reached him clearly.

She beckoned to Kai. 'Come with me, my child, and I will take you to my beautiful palace in the land of ice and snow.'

The boy obeyed and the sledge took a careful turn of the stage under Steph's expert steering from the wings.

'Creep into my warm fur,' said the Snow Queen, tucking the polar bear around Kai and kissing him on the forehead so that he fell under her spell and the glass splinters in his heart and eyes turned to ice. 'I will take care of you for ever and ever.'

The sledge took another turn and disappeared off stage. The Colonel joined in the clapping.

The rehearsal went on.

Gerda set off in search of Kai, encountering an enchantress with a garden of talking flowers, a black raven who befriended her and a prince and princess. As she travelled through a dark forest she was captured by cruel robbers. Fortunately, an obliging reindeer helped her escape and carried her on his back all the way to Lapland where a wise old woman – the part indignantly declined by Mrs Pudsey – sent them on to another wise old woman in Finland who told her that Kai was being kept in the ice palace of the Snow Queen.

Conveniently, the Snow Queen decided to go off on a visit to warmer countries and turn them cold (cue for a dramatic reappearance of the polar bear sledge and the delivery of another chilling line from Joan). A barefoot, very cold and very weary Gerda arrived at last at the ice palace to be set upon by the snowflake guards and then rescued by angels who fought the guards off with their spears. Inside the palace, Gerda discovered Kai alone in the empty hall. When she hugged him, her tears of joy melted the ice in his heart and washed away the ice splinter from his eye, so that he was his old and kind self again. Before long, they were back home where the town church bells were ringing and it was summer with flowers in full bloom. Gerda delivered the final words.

'Our roses bloom and fade away,
Our Infant Lord abides always;
May we be blessed His face to see,
And ever little children be.'

The Colonel had more or less followed the story and thought it should please all the young members of the audience, though it seemed a bit of a pity that the Snow Queen hadn't got more of her just deserts at the end, rather than just going off to have fun.

Joan Dryden came up to him. 'I must say your sledge was very comfortable, Hugh.'

He smiled. 'All thanks to the bear.'

'Where on earth did it come from?'

'My neighbour's attic. Her great uncle shot it.'

'Well, I'm glad he did. I wouldn't have liked to meet the animal when it was still alive. Was I all right, do you think?'

'You were better than all right.'

'Thank you, Hugh. You always know what to say. Actually, I'm rather enjoying myself. Mrs Cuthbertson has told me to choose my own costume from some local hirers, but if they don't have anything up to scratch I'll get one from London.

It will be rather fun dressing up. Do you know that woman standing over there? She's just told me she'll be doing my make-up.'

'Her name's Thora Jay. She used to be a professional make-up artist. She's meant to be very good.'

'We'll see. I know something about make-up myself, as you can imagine. She doesn't exactly inspire confidence, does she? Look at her!'

'Looks can be deceptive.'

'Oh, do you think so, Hugh? I disagree. Looks tell you everything about a person. If people look dull and ordinary it's usually because they are.'

The sledge was stowed away in the room off the stage and Steph gave the Colonel, Naomi and the polar bear a lift home in the pickup truck. Marjorie Cuthbertson, recognizing Steph's superior sledge-pulling skills, had lost no time in co-opting him as an honorary Player. He seemed rather embarrassed about it.

'I hope you don't mind, Colonel? After all, it's your sledge.'

'And they're your wheels, Steph. I'd much sooner you were in charge of them. Safer for everyone.'

Since it was already Chivas Regal time, he carried the polar bear into Pond Cottage and lowered him into a corner of the sitting room while Naomi prised Thursday off his cushion.

The Colonel lit the log fire and fetched the Scotch. 'Good health, Naomi.'

'Same to you, Hugh. Well, I think that went jolly well, don't you? Your sledge is a winner.'

'Thanks to your great uncle's polar bear.'

'He certainly helped. Hardly any forgotten lines, for once, and I must say I thought Joan was rather good. By the time we've got scenery and costumes and make-up, everything's going to come together quite well. I hope Bob Fox does a decent job with the lighting. He says he's got big plans for the Northern Lights when they get to Lapland. All the colours flickering away.'

'How about sound effects?'

'Lavinia Warner always does those. Remember her from the fête bric-a-brac stall? We've got a wind machine for the blizzard scenes – you just turn a handle and it shrieks and moans like anything. Sounds just like the real thing. She's jolly good at doing horse's hooves with coconuts too, though, of course, we don't need those this time.'

'Any music?'

'Some new chap in the village has taken that on. He's going to play suitable snatches of Sibelius. All very Nordic.'

'No sing-a-longs?'

'Definitely not. Marjorie has vetoed any of the panto stuff. By the way, Ruth and Tom are inviting all the village to the Manor after the last performance. Mince pies and mulled wine.'

'All the village? That's kind of them.'

'Yes, isn't it? It was always the tradition every Christmas when Sir Alan was alive, then Ursula dropped it like a hot potato as soon as he died. Didn't want us riff-raff in the house fingering the curtains, I suppose. Anyway, Ruth has revived it now that Ursula's no longer with us and she's married Tom. Thank God she's nothing like her mother. Just think, if Tom hadn't turned up to be our GP in Frog End, Ruth might have sold the Manor when her mother got bumped off and people like the Drydens could have bought it. Unthinkable as well as unimaginable.'

The Colonel agreed that it was hard to picture Kenneth and Joan Dryden playing the Manor role with any enthusiasm, and very unlikely that invitations would have been forthcoming en masse at Christmas. 'I'll look forward to the party.'

'We muck in, of course. People make mince pies to take. Enough to go round.'

'Could I buy some instead?'

'They're supposed to be home-made. It's part of the tradition too, which means some are very good and others are inedible. It's the thought that counts. Anyway, people only eat a token one. Don't worry, Hugh, you can take some wine to be mulled instead. That's always welcome. Do you realize that it'll soon be Christmas?'

He realized very well because Susan had reminded him when she had rung that morning.

'You will be coming to us, won't you, Father? The children will be so disappointed if you don't. It's Eric's school carol

service on the sixteenth. If you're here by then, you can come
to it.'

Grandfathers, he knew, were meant to do exactly that sort
of thing: go to school carol services and concerts and plays
and stand on touchlines, cheering. He had missed out on most
of it with Marcus and Alison because he had spent so much
time serving abroad while they had been at boarding school
in England.

'Unfortunately I can't, Susan. I'm so sorry. The village is
putting on a Christmas play during that week and I'm supposed
to be helping with the scenery.'

'Do you have to, Father? I'd have thought that family should
come first during the festive season.'

She was absolutely right, of course. He had felt very guilty.

When Naomi's other half drink was finished, he offered to
carry the polar bear over to her cottage.

'Would you mind keeping the wretched thing here, Hugh?
It upsets the dogs. They keep barking at it.'

He wasn't surprised. Two Jack Russells would have made
a nice snack for the bear when he was alive.

Thursday had gone off to the kitchen to have his Munchies
supper and, in his absence, the Colonel made the bear comfortable on the sofa, laying him on his back, head supported by
the armrest, front paws placed neatly together and rear paws
propped up against the arm at the other end. He sat down to
drink the remains of his whisky and, presently, Thursday
returned. Cats, he knew, were very good at summing up a new
situation at a glance and judging if it was to their advantage
or otherwise. It only took a moment for the decision to be
reached. Thursday jumped up on to the sofa and settled down
between the bear's front paws, kneading the thick white fur
with his claws. He blinked his eyes once or twice at the
Colonel. He even purred.

TWELVE

The dress rehearsal of *The Snow Queen* took place three days before the first performance, with full costume, make-up, scenery, props, lighting and music.

The Major, who had somehow managed to avoid attending most of the previous rehearsals, found himself kept busy hauling things around behind the scenes. The fake rose trees in the kindly old grandmother's summer garden kept keeling over and shedding their paper petals, and the real Christmas trees, standing about in buckets and sprayed with glitter on one side for winter, were damned prickly to manoeuvre.

Bloody stupid idea of Flora Bentley's, he thought. Typical of the woman. No consideration at all. He had neither forgotten, nor forgiven, the time when she had argued with him at the summer fête committee meeting over the allocation of trestle tables. She had taken three of them for her cakes while he had been left with only one for the bottle stall. She'd even had the nerve to tell him that there shouldn't be a bottle stall at all. Drinking shouldn't be encouraged, she'd said, as though there were rows of Johnny Walker and Smirnoff and Gordons instead of the cheap British sherry and the homemade wines that were usually donated. During his several years' tenure of the fête bottle stall, he had discovered that people would make wine out of the most extraordinary things – peapods, parsnips, nettles, dandelions, gorse, turnips . . . old socks, he shouldn't wonder, if they found some lying about.

Luckily, the Colonel was there, lending a dependable hand. He was a good sort of chap to have on your side when the going got tough. No slacking or anything like that. Poor old Toby Jugge had wanted to help but Marjorie had spotted him hanging around the dressing room and sent him packing. It was damned unfair. He was still a member of the Players, after all.

The Major waited in the wings as the two children pretended to play together in the kindly old grandmother's garden. Boring as anything, in his opinion. Not a patch on *Puss in Boots* last year. Or had it been *Cinderella*? Still, everyone seemed to be remembering their lines, more or less, and the snow-capped mountains on the back cloth strung up behind the Christmas trees looked all right from a distance.

The curtains rattled across at the end of the first scene, one of them sticking halfway so that he had to climb on a chair and free it. Time to cart the rose trees off and turn the bloody Christmas trees round to their glittery winter side. More damned prickles. His hands and face were as sore as hell.

As the next scene opened, the boy, whose name the Major had forgotten, was pretending to play with some other village boys, throwing cotton wool snowballs at each other. One of them hit the Major on the head – aimed deliberately, he reckoned. He shook his fist. Little tykes.

The lighting went down and Lavinia Warner started cranking up her wind machine to blizzard strength, drowning out the taped music composed by some Finnish chap. Cue for the Snow Queen to show up.

He waited expectantly. According to Marjorie, Joan Dryden had insisted on her costume being hired from London. The old girl had been furious about it.

'She's expecting the Players to pay and it's far more than we can afford. Quite unnecessary.'

Mrs Dryden had also insisted on having a corner of the communal dressing room curtained off for herself, which had left even less room for the other players to change in. There had been a lot of muttering and grumbling, but the old girl couldn't do much about that either, or about the full-length mirror that had been installed for Her Majesty's private use. Or about the make-up woman taking ten times as long over the Snow Queen as the other leads, closeted with her behind the apartheid curtain.

Two spotlights, one on each side of the stage, came on and the Snow Queen rolled slowly into view on her sledge, reclining on the polar bear skin. The Major caught his breath. Whatever the London costumier was charging, it was worth every damned penny. The glittering crown, the filmy cloak draped over a gown that looked as though it was made of frozen snowflakes.

And the queen's face, framed by long silver tresses, might have been carved from ice. Hats off to that make-up woman, whatever her name was! As the sledge advanced smoothly, followed on foot by the bedazzled boy, the queen sprinkled handfuls of silver dust around and beckoned seductively to him. No surprise that the lad jumped to it, the Major thought wistfully. At his age, he'd have gone like a shot.

The first two performances were matinées. The audiences were either very young or very old and the Snow Queen made a big impression on everybody.

The Colonel, on scene-shifting duty backstage, saw rows of gaping mouths whenever she appeared. The London costume was sensational and the queen's icy make-up a work of art. Thora Jay certainly knew her job. Even Joan had acknowledged it.

'I looked rather fabulous, didn't I, Hugh?'

'Extremely.'

'And Thora's not quite as dull and boring as I thought. We got on rather well, as a matter of fact. Chatting away like old friends. I practically told her my life story.'

'Did she tell you hers?'

'No, I wasn't interested. But she knew a lot of luvvy gossip. She had some amusing tales to tell about actors she'd worked with.'

The third and final performance of *The Snow Queen* started in the early evening, attended by the rest of the village. After the queen's dramatic appearance on the sledge, accompanied by piercing wolf whistles, the audience lapsed into silence. This time, the Colonel saw bored faces and stifled yawns. The valiant efforts of Gerda to find and rescue Kai went unappreciated until the scene where she entered the dark forest – the haunt of the robbers. As she stopped, centre stage, looking fearfully left and right, a polar bear emerged from behind one of the potted Christmas trees. Someone in the audience immediately shouted out: 'He's behind you!'

Everyone woke up. There were roars of laughter as the bear dodged back behind the tree and more warning shouts when he reappeared from another tree and crept up to the girl.

'He's behind you! *Behind you!*'

As soon as Gerda turned round to look, the bear vanished again and so the game went on until the robbers arrived.

The audience hissed the dastardly robbers, clapped the helpful reindeer, oohed and aahed at the flickering multi-coloured Northern Lights, booed the evil Snow Queen in her ice palace, cheered on the winged angels in their fight with the villainous snowflake guards, gave exaggerated sighs when Gerda's tears melted Kai's icy heart and eyes, clapped the happy ending back at the kindly old grandmother's house and whooped and whistled and stamped the floor with their feet as the cast took their bows. There were calls for the polar bear, but in vain.

'I've no idea who it was,' the Major said, all hurt innocence. 'I was busy moving things around.'

Drawn up to her full height, chest inflated like a wartime pilot's Mae West, the old girl could be a frightening sight. Boadicea on the warpath, luckily without the helmet and the chariot – and the knives.

'Do you really expect me to believe that, Roger? Of course it was your Mr Jugge. It was just the sort of thing he'd do. His idea of a joke. And you must have encouraged him.'

'I did nothing of the sort.'

'I hope you realize that he ruined the whole final perfor-mance. Wrecked everything.'

'Well, the audience seemed to enjoy themselves.'

'I dare say they did. They thought it was supposed to be just another rowdy pantomime when it was intended to be a serious and uplifting story of the triumph of good against evil. I blame you for letting that happen, Roger.'

The Major sighed. There was no justice. He'd no idea who had been under the polar bear skin – obviously filched at some point from the Snow Queen's sledge – but the finger pointed to old Toby, it had to be said. He'd seen him hanging round backstage. If so, he'd done it damned well. The bear had looked alive, and the audience had come to life, too. Everyone had had a good laugh and there was nothing wrong with that. Not much else to laugh about, these days.

Oh well, at least there was the mulled wine and mince pie bash at the Manor to come. He didn't care about the mince pies – couldn't stand the things – but the mulled wine should warm the old cockles.

There was a large Christmas tree in the oak-panelled entrance hall of the Manor. The Colonel admired it as he arrived. It was as a Christmas tree should be, decorated with old-fashioned multi-coloured glass lights, proper ornaments and with a big silver star at the top. No tinsel, no plastic, no fake snow and no blinking and winking.

Ruth was welcoming everyone. He thought she looked well and happy and was glad for her. She had gone through a terrible time when her mother had been murdered, and there had also been a long and unhappy affair with a married man. Tom Harvey had saved the situation, and now there was the good news of the April baby.

She took his arm. 'Thank goodness you're here, Hugh. I need your help. Tom's been called out urgently and I don't know when he'll be back.'

'How can I help?'

'Well, you could serve the mulled wine, if you don't mind? Tom made a vat of it with all sorts of lovely spices and it's on the Aga keeping warm. The glasses are out on trays.'

'Of course.' He held up his bottle of wine. 'Will this be any use?'

She smiled. 'I shouldn't be surprised. Thank you.'

He went into the kitchen, ladled the mulled wine into the glasses and carried a tray into the crowded drawing room, working his way round. The mince pies were being offered as he did so and he could see that Naomi had been right about their varying standards. Mrs Peabody, a widow well into her nineties, thrust a shaky platter at him, mincemeat oozing from pallid pastry.

'Do have one, Colonel. I made them myself.'

Luckily, both his hands were fully occupied.

The Drydens were standing by the log fire, Joan holding court to a group of admirers. The glacial Snow Queen make-up had gone and she was wearing bright red lipstick. She took a glass from the tray. 'How was I, Hugh?'

'Better than ever.'

'It's all been rather amusing, I must say.'

'You didn't mind the boos and hisses this evening?'

'Oh, no. It made it much more fun. Who was the bear?'

'I don't know. It's a mystery.'

'Well, he certainly livened things up.'

'Did your daughter enjoy the play?'

'Clarissa would never enjoy anything involving me. She refused point blank to go to it, just as she refused to come here. We left her at home where she's probably snorting coke.'

He moved on with the tray, encountering Naomi with her own plate of mince pies, which looked a great improvement on Mrs Peabody's.

'I hear you're standing in for Tom, Hugh.'

'I'm doing my best.'

'Well, save some mulled wine for me. Look at Monica Pudsey over there. She's still in a big sulk over not being cast as the Snow Queen.'

He glanced over his shoulder. 'So I see.'

'If looks could kill,' Naomi said, 'Joan would be dead.'

'Luckily, they don't.'

He went back to the kitchen to fill more glasses and then more glasses after that, until everybody had one.

Thora Jay crossed his path. 'A mince pie, Colonel?'

He took one from the three-tiered cake plate that she was holding aloft by its handle.

'Thank you, Mrs Jay. They look wonderful.'

They did, indeed, with sugar-dusted pastry stars on top of the mincemeat. Irresistible.

'You did a first-class job with the make-up,' he said. 'And the Snow Queen was an amazing sight. She looked as though she was really made of ice. How on earth did you manage it?'

'Tricks of the trade, like I told you. The lighting helped too. Bob Fox and I worked it out together.'

He took the empty tray back to the kitchen once more, poured himself a glass of the mulled wine and ate the mince pie. He hadn't tasted one in years. Laura used to make them for past Christmases, even when they were stationed in the tropics. He could remember her mixing up the mincemeat several weeks beforehand and putting it into jars. Dried fruit and spices, brown sugar, shredded suet and a hefty slug of brandy, if his memory served him correctly. Despite the name, no meat – minced or otherwise.

Ruth came into the kitchen. 'Tom just rang. He says he won't be back for ages. The patient's in a bad way. Do you mind carrying on as bartender, Hugh?'

'Not at all. Shall I add some more wine to the mix?'

'Good idea.'

He poured in the bottle he had brought, stirring it over a low heat. When it was warm enough, he ladled some into a jug and did another tour of the drawing room, refilling empty glasses. The Major's, for one. He looked as though he needed it.

'I'm in the dog house with Marjorie. She thinks I put Toby Jugge up to doing the bear thing. Fact is I didn't.'

The Colonel smiled. 'Well, whoever it was, he was very good.'

'Did you see Toby in last year's show?'

'I'm afraid not.'

'He was the Dame. Brought the house down. Good old Toby.'

There was a sudden commotion over by the fireplace. Trouble of some kind? The Colonel, forcing his way through the crowd, found Joan Dryden collapsed on the floor, choking and clawing at her throat. She lay gasping for breath, her face red, her eyes swollen, her body twitching in violent spasms.

Kenneth Dryden was on his knees beside her. He looked up at the Colonel. 'She's in anaphylactic shock. It must have been something she ate. Where the hell's her handbag? Her EpiPen will be in it.'

The black bag was found on a chair. Kenneth Dryden wrenched it open and tipped it upside down, shaking it hard so that all the contents fell out: lipstick, scent, comb, purse, keys, tissues, mirror, hand cream, hairbrush. He thrust his hand deep into the bag. 'Christ, it's not there! Call an ambulance, Hugh! And tell them to hurry, for God's sake!'

*   *   *

The rest of the guests had left, but the Colonel and Naomi stayed with Ruth, waiting for Tom's return.

'I'm responsible,' she kept saying in anguish. 'It's all my fault.'

The Colonel made her sit down. 'It's nothing of the kind, Ruth. According to Kenneth Dryden, Joan was allergic to nuts. But you weren't to know that. There were none in the mulled wine and it seems unlikely there were any in the mince pies.'

'There could have been,' Naomi said. 'Some mincemeat recipes have almonds. I used to make it with them myself. Not now, though – they're too expensive. Of course, I don't know about the others. People use different recipes with all sorts of ingredients. What was that pen thing that Kenneth Dryden was on about?'

'EpiPen,' Ruth said. 'Tom always carries one in his bag. It's for treating people in allergic shock. You use it to inject them with adrenaline. If Mrs Dryden was severely allergic she would always keep one with her so she could inject herself in an emergency, or somebody else could do it for her.'

Naomi frowned. 'Well, she must have forgotten it this time. Or maybe she didn't see any good reason to bring it. Mince pies would seem harmless enough.'

'If only Tom had been here, he could have treated her at once.'

The Colonel put a steadying hand on Ruth's shoulder. 'The hospital will be taking good care of her. And her husband is with her. She'll be all right.'

But Joan Dryden died during the night. The news was all round the village by morning. Her death was reported in the local newspaper the following day.

FORMER TOP MODEL TAKEN ILL AT VILLAGE CHRISTMAS GATHERING.

Joan Lowe, who has died in hospital, was a famous model in the eighties. She had recently moved into a six-bedroomed period house in Frog End village with her husband, Kenneth Dryden, the former TV travel documentary maker turned chat show host. She played the starring part of the Snow Queen in the village amateur dramatic society's Christmas play this week, and to much acclaim. It is understood that she suffered from an allergy to nuts, and this is believed to have been the cause of her tragic death.

The accompanying photograph had been taken many years ago, at the height of her career, and showed Joan at her very best. At least, the Colonel thought soberly, she would have been pleased about that.

THIRTEEN

M iss Butler had been greatly shocked by Mrs Dryden's death.

Of course, she had not been well known in the village, nor well-liked, though some people had been rather dazzled by her. But it was still a terrible thing to have happened, and just before Christmas, too.

It had been dreadful to see Mrs Dryden in such a pitiful state, choking and unable to get her breath. If Dr Harvey had not been out on a call, he could certainly have done something. The Colonel had immediately sent for an ambulance but it had seemed to take a very long time to arrive.

Apparently, a post-mortem had confirmed that the mince pie she had eaten at the Manor had contained a considerable number of almonds, causing the fatal allergic reaction. Flora Bentley, whose nephew was a senior hospital consultant, and therefore constantly quoted as an authority on all medical matters, had been able to provide some interesting information about allergies. Nuts, insect stings, shell fish, sesame seeds and soya beans could all be deadly – even some plants. A beautiful purple flower called monkshood, growing freely in English country gardens, was highly poisonous if you so much as brushed against it. A frightening thought. Somehow, one never imagined such things existing in England's green and pleasant land.

Poor Ruth had been very upset – so unfortunate in her delicate condition. She had blamed herself for the tragedy, but that was nonsense. Nobody was to blame – not even the person who had offered Mrs Dryden the mince pie in question, because how could they have known about her allergy? She had never told anybody in the village about it, so far as was known. Miss Butler had never made mince pies herself and she had no idea of their contents. Cooking had never been her strong suit. There had been no requirement for it during her time spent in the WRNS and the meals she prepared now for herself were only of the simplest kind. Poached eggs on toast, a sardine salad, sometimes a small lamb chop as a treat. She thanked God that she had not been responsible for the fatal mince pie. It had been one of Mrs Jay's, apparently. She herself had seen Mrs Dryden take one, and very delicious it had looked.

She felt sorry for poor Mr Dryden. His wife's death must have been a dreadful blow. To make matters worse, Mrs Dryden could, it seemed, easily have been saved by the emergency syringe which was so disastrously missing from her handbag that evening. An EpiPen, Mr Dryden had called it. It was not something Miss Butler had ever heard of.

Thinking about it later, Miss Butler recalled the time when Mrs Dryden had searched through her capacious bag at the read-through rehearsal in the village hall. Black suede, if she was not mistaken, and very expensive-looking. Mrs Dryden had been hunting for her spectacles and she had taken all sorts of things out of the bag and piled them on the table. It was astonishing what some women carried around with them. Her own handbag, rather like she imagined the Queen's to be, contained very little: a handkerchief, a powder compact, a mirror and a comb. The Queen would probably carry a lipstick, too, but she herself never wore it. Lipstick had not been encouraged in the WRNS and her father, the Admiral, had vehemently disapproved of it, though he had once remarked that it was a different matter for the Queen. Part of the Queen's duty was to wear make-up, he had considered, in order to stand out from the crowd for her loyal subjects.

Miss Butler had not been sitting at the table for the first read-through at the village hall, having no speaking part in the play, but her chair had been close enough for her to see Mrs Dryden's handbag clutter and, among it, she had happened to notice a strange tube-shaped object, blue at one end and orange at the other. Now, she realized that it must have been the vital EpiPen. Other people could have noticed it as well, especially those round the table, and probably wondered what it was. Or had they known?

Miss Butler made herself a cup of tea and sat down by the gas fire in her sitting room. It was all very disturbing. There was the daughter to consider, too, as well as Mr Dryden. Not a very appealing child, from all accounts, but she would surely be grief-stricken at losing her mother. You only had one mother in life, and though Freda Butler had only the haziest memory of hers, she had always felt the loss.

The funeral was to take place in London, so it was understood, and would doubtless be well-attended by celebrities who would dress as though they were going to a party. Nobody seemed to wear black at funerals any more, which she found quite shocking. There was no respect. No sense of decorum. Anything went at funerals these days. People wore jeans or very short dresses with very low necklines. Even shorts. They wore loud colours, tottering shoes, clumsy sports trainers, and almost never hats. Even more shocking to her than the clothes was the curious modern custom of placing bunches of flowers wherever some unfortunate death had taken place, and very often by people who had never met or known the person or people in question. She had seen them left beside a road where a traffic accident had occurred, and whenever there had been some terrible disaster the newspapers showed photographs of flowers laid down by strangers for strangers. It seemed to have begun when the Princess of Wales had died so tragically and there had been not only a sea of flowers left outside the palace but scenes of uncontrolled and hysterical behaviour, usually only to be seen in foreign countries. Miss Butler had greatly admired the Royal Family's dignified and calm restraint, especially in the face of vulgar and offensive criticism in the newspapers.

It was also understood that Hassels was to be sold. An estate agent had already been observed calling at the house and photographs had been taken. It was rumoured that the asking price was considerably more than Mr Dryden had paid only a few months ago, but there had been expensive improvements.

As Freda Butler sipped her tea, another thought occurred to her. Had the missing EpiPen ever been found? And, if so, where?

The Colonel had resumed work on the wooden rocking horse. There was no hope of it being ready in time for

Christmas, but luckily his granddaughter was too young to mind. The excitement of Father Christmas coming down the chimney still lay in the future.

When Marjorie Cuthbertson had interrupted him previously, he had been in the middle of tracing the paper pattern for the horse's head and had almost reached the mouth. The project had been laid aside to make room and time for the Snow Queen's sledge but was now reinstated on the workbench. This time he had finished tracing round the head and was starting to saw along the biro outline when there was a knock on the shed door. The Colonel swore under his breath. Naomi? Flora Bentley? Miss Butler? No, she would never come to the shed. Mrs Cuthbertson again with another request? God forbid!

It was none of them.

Kenneth Dryden said, 'I tried your front door but there was no answer. Then I came round the side and saw your shed. You look busy.'

He lied politely. 'Not at all. What can I do for you?'

'I wanted to thank you for your help when Joan was taken ill.'

'I'm only sorry I couldn't have done more.'

'You did your best. May I come in for a moment?'

'Yes, of course.'

He opened the door wider. Men were different. They didn't touch things, or pry or ask a lot of questions. They understood sheds. It was a male conspiracy.

'Nice place you've got here. I've always rather liked the idea of having a bolthole where I could get some peace.' Kenneth Dryden nodded towards the workbench. 'I used to do a bit of woodwork myself, many years ago. Very therapeutic.'

'I'm only a beginner.'

'Well, you did a very good job with the sledge you made for Joan. She enjoyed the whole experience, you know. Especially that last performance.'

'She was extremely good.'

'Yes, she was, wasn't she? Of course, the part suited her down to the ground. What's that you're making?'

'It's supposed to be a rocking horse for my granddaughter

but I haven't got very far. I hope she doesn't grow up before I finish it.'

'Well, I'm sorry to have interrupted you. I imagine you've heard that I'm moving back to London and selling the house?'

'Not much goes unnoticed in Frog End.'

'So I gather. Clarissa has already gone back to London and I'm going to buy her a flat there. I don't think we'd get on very well on our own. She hated her mother, you know, and she's pleased that she's dead. Thrilled, in fact.'

'I'm sure that's not really so.'

'Unfortunately, it is. Do you mind if I ask your opinion about something, Hugh? In confidence.'

People often confided in him. The Colonel had no idea why. 'I'm afraid I'm as fallacious as the next man.'

'I'd value your judgement.'

There was a pause and the Colonel waited resignedly.

Kenneth Dryden said, 'After Joan died, I looked everywhere for that missing EpiPen. I wanted to know what had happened to it. When I drove her to the village hall for that last performance, she was wearing the dress she wore later for the Manor party and carrying that same bag. It was one of her favourites. I searched in the car at first, thinking that the Pen had somehow fallen out of the bag on the way.'

'Or perhaps she had forgotten to take it?'

'That did happen, but rarely. She knew how important it was to have one with her at all times. In fact, she was supposed to take two EpiPens, in case one of them didn't work, but she never did. She said they took up too much room. Her "stupid Pens", she called them, and she hated having to depend on them. The spare one was kept on a shelf in the bathroom at Hassels and it was still there when I searched the house later. I went back to the Manor and Mrs Harvey was good enough to help me hunt. And I searched the room off the stage where Joan had changed in and out of her costume. Nothing either. She had a third Pen which was always kept in our flat in London and when I was there for the funeral, I checked and found it in her bedside drawer, as usual. But the other one – the one that should have been in her bag at the Manor – has completely vanished. I think someone took it, Hugh.'

'What for?'

'To harm Joan.'

'But who would want to do that?'

'Clarissa, for one. She hated her mother enough to wish her dead. She told me so. In fact, she said that if I didn't buy her a flat so she could leave home, she'd find a way to kill her.'

'Teenagers say all sorts of things they don't really mean.'

'Oh, I think she meant it, all right. I think she took the Pen out of the bag before Joan and I left for the village hall that evening and that she did so deliberately. With malice aforethought – I believe that's the correct legal phrase – which, incidentally, makes it murder. She knew all about the mulled wine and the mince pies, you see. It was written on our invitation.'

'But she couldn't possibly have known that any of the mince pies would contain almonds. As I understand it, most recipes don't.'

'Christmas and nuts go together, don't they? It can be enough to eat something that's been anywhere near nuts if you are very allergic – which Joan was. Food manufacturers print clear warnings about that on their packaging, but it's always risky when the food has been cooked by someone else. We had a few scares over the years, with Joan ending up in hospital. She always claimed she'd never be able to use an EpiPen on herself, though it's actually very easy. I've done it for her twice. You just take the safety cap off and push it hard against the thigh and the Pen does the rest automatically. I made sure I knew exactly what to do. If that EpiPen had been in her bag, she would be alive today.'

The Colonel frowned. 'I wonder why she risked eating the mince pie.'

'Joan hadn't a clue about cooking ingredients. We always ate out in in places where her allergy was known and understood, or we had special meals delivered to the flat. I would have stopped her eating the mince pie if I'd seen her take it, but I had my back turned, talking to other people. I blame myself for that, but I hold Clarissa responsible. I think she took the EpiPen from the bag and threw it away somewhere. And it all happened exactly as she had hoped. So, my question to you is do you think I should confront my daughter or should I go to the police?'

The question was easily answered. 'Neither. You would be making a terrible mistake. You have no proof that your daughter did any such thing, or had any such intent.'

'My instinct tells me she did.'

'Instinct is unreliable.'

'So, I do nothing?'

'Your wife's death was the result of tragic mischance, Kenneth. Nothing else. You're not thinking rationally. Bereavement can play havoc with the mind – I know that from my own experience.'

There was silence for a moment.

'When did your wife die, Hugh?'

'Twelve years ago.'

'Do you still miss her?'

'Every day. But I've had to learn to live without her.'

'I left my first wife for Joan, you know. Xanthe committed suicide. Hanged herself. It was ghastly. The gossip columns blamed Joan, as though she had lured me away. The truth is I went very willingly.'

'Was Joan married too?'

'Divorced. Twice over, as a matter of fact. But our marriage lasted for nearly twenty years. I think it surprised everybody. Joan was in a class of her own – you saw that for yourself. An extremely beautiful and extraordinary woman. Very expensive to run, and sometimes impossible to deal with, but never, ever dull. I can't say that she was the perfect, doting mother, because she wasn't, but then Clarissa was always difficult from the day she was born. We sent her to a child psychologist but all that did was cost us a great deal of money. In fact, if anything, it made her worse.' Kenneth Dryden was silent for another moment. 'Very well, I'll take your advice, Hugh, and do nothing, but I'll still go on believing that Clarissa took the EpiPen. Unless, of course, you can find out who else did or where it is now.' He took a card out of his pocket. 'Here's my number in London. Call me if you do, then maybe I'll change my mind.'

After his visitor had left, the Colonel went back to the rocking horse and finished sawing round the head. That done, he spent some time sanding away the marks and smoothing the edges, and while he did so he thought about his bizarre conversation with Kenneth Dryden.

The man seemed convinced that his daughter had contrived her mother's death, which was patently absurd. Clarissa had not gone to either the last performance of *The Snow Queen* or to the party at the Manor afterwards. Even if she had taken the EpiPen out of Joan's bag earlier, on some wild impulse, she could not possibly have arranged for her mother to eat a mince pie containing almonds rather than one without. At least a dozen women had been circulating at the Manor party, bearing all kinds of homemade mince pies – from Mrs Peabody's shaky platter of disasters to Mrs Jay's sugar-dusted stars. A few with almonds, but most, apparently, without and perfectly harmless. There had been no way of telling them apart and no warning could have been given to Joan since nobody had, apparently, been aware of her allergy to nuts.

The EpiPen had somehow been mislaid or forgotten – not so surprising, given Joan's apparent aversion to having to carry her 'stupid Pens' around. If Tom Harvey had not been called out to a patient and at home instead, he would have been able to treat Joan immediately. Her death had been the result of a chain of bad luck. Nothing more and nothing less.

He remembered his own state of mind after Laura's death. A black pit of grief and loneliness and bitterness. Sleepless nights, empty days. It had taken years for him to get a proper grip on life again. Given time, Kenneth Dryden would see things differently.

He continued working on the rocking horse, tracing round the main body next, sawing along the biro line, sanding and smoothing. Dryden had described woodwork as therapeutic and it was certainly an absorbing task. But he found himself going over his conversation with Dryden in his mind.

It was certainly odd that the EpiPen had vanished into thin air. If he remembered correctly, the bag had been a deep one with a drawstring closure at the top. Dryden had had to wrench it wide open before he could shake out the contents. It seemed almost impossible that the Pen could have fallen out by accident. And he thought of the bright red lipstick that Joan had been wearing at the Manor. She must have retrieved it from her bag to apply after her ice-white Snow Queen make-up had been removed. Wouldn't she have noticed then if the EpiPen was missing? If Clarissa had already taken it. No, on second thoughts, given the muddle of the contents, very possibly not. But someone else could have taken it in the backstage dressing room at the village hall, or perhaps later when the bag had been lying on the chair at the Manor party? Except that the Frog End Players were hardly a gang of petty thieves and the EpiPen was of no use to anybody else other than Joan Dryden. If it had been removed then it must have been by someone who not only intended to cause her deliberate harm but who had also somehow seen to it that she had taken a mince pie containing nuts.

I'll still go on believing that Clarissa took the EpiPen. Unless, of course, you can find out who else did or where it is now.

The Colonel stopped sanding and smoothing.

Not only who and where, he thought, but when? And why?

FOURTEEN

The Major had run Toby Jugge to earth in a corner of the Dog and Duck. He prodded him in the chest.

'Come on, old chap. Spill the beans. It was you, wasn't it?'

'Me what?'

'Don't play the innocent. You were under that polar bear skin. Gave us all a jolly good laugh, but Marjorie's been giving me hell ever since. She thinks I put you up to it.'

'How does she know it was me?'

'She's got seven senses.'

'But no proof.'

'She doesn't need any.'

'Well, something had to be done, Roger. The audience were falling asleep and I woke them up. That old routine never fails. He's behind you! Been doing it for years. They love it.'

'Didn't anybody see you take the bear skin?'

'Not a soul.'

'What about Mrs Dryden?'

'Her Majesty was closeted in her private dressing room having her make-up titivated, and I'd got the fur back on the sledge by the time she came out from behind her curtain to do the last scene at the palace. I have to hand it to her. The play was a yawner but she wasn't. Damned bad luck what happened to her afterwards.'

Marjorie had seemed to blame him for that too, though it couldn't possibly have been his fault. Or anybody else's, come to that. As old Toby had said, it had been a case of damned bad luck.

He could remember the same sort of thing happening to a chap he'd known out East who'd trodden on a snake by mistake and got bitten on the ankle. A harmless sort of snake; not even very big. But the chap had turned out to be highly allergic to snake venom and snuffed it. An unlucky throw of the dice,

you might say. Fortune's wheel spinning against you. An
unexpected twist of fate. One man's meat was another man's
poison, though who would have imagined it of a mince pie?
He'd never heard of such a thing. People must eat millions of
them at Christmas without any ill effect whatsoever.

He sighed. All in all, it was looking like it was going to be
a pretty bleak Christmas. The only bright spot was that
Marjorie's sister was going on a cruise this year and would
not be visiting as usual. She had wanted them to go with her
but, thank God, the old girl felt the same about cruises as he
did. Cooped up with hundreds of people you'd never met
before, going somewhere you didn't want to go to. Being
seasick, catching some horrible bug and all the rest of it. Of
course, there was always the faint chance that he might run
into some talent on board, but he doubted it. So far as he could
see, cruise ships were like Noah's Ark. The passengers travelled
two by two. Besides, with Marjorie never far away there
wouldn't be much scope for action.

He roused himself with an effort. It didn't do to get down-
in-the mouth at this time of year. He must pull himself together.
Look merry. Brace up.

'What's yours, Toby?'

'Same as usual, old friend.'

'Make that two doubles,' he said to the landlord.

As the Colonel walked up the Manor drive, he saw Tom
Harvey's car parked outside the house and the young doctor
coming out of the front door.

'Hallo, Hugh. I'm just off on my rounds but Ruth's at home,
if you'd like to see her.'

'I was wondering if she was feeling brighter?'

'About Mrs Dryden, you mean? Yes, I think she's recovered
all right. You were a great help, Hugh.'

'I'm afraid all I did was lift the phone.'

'You were also a very steadying influence, by all accounts.
Thanks for that. I wish to God I'd been there.'

'Could you have saved her?'

'Almost certainly.' Tom patted the bag he was carrying. 'I
always keep EpiPens with me for emergencies. Anaphylactic

shock can come on very fast and there's no time to waste. In effect, Mrs Dryden was poisoned and, unfortunately for her, it was deadly.'

'I suppose the EpiPen hasn't turned up?'

'No. Ruth said she and Mr Dryden looked everywhere here for it, but no luck. They do go missing sometimes, you know, just like other things. Or people get a bit less careful. You're looking fit and well these days, Hugh. Still alive and kicking. You'll find Ruth in one of the greenhouses. I know she'd like to see you.'

It was Tom Harvey who had got him through the early days in Frog End when he had been doubtful if life was worth living, dispensing common sense and sympathy rather than drugs.

The Colonel waved as he drove off. He walked round the side of the Manor, across the frosty lawn where the fête was held in summer and on to the greenhouses beside the walled kitchen garden. There were four of them, all large, old and beautiful and in need of expensive repair and maintenance. Ruth, he knew, was determined to keep them going rather than replace them with cheaper, modern alternatives and he applauded her for it. He found her in the one furthest away, bent over ranks of seed trays and so absorbed in her task that it was several minutes before she saw him.

'Hugh! How long have you been standing there?'

'Not long. I didn't want to disturb you.'

'I'm glad you did. It's fiddly work and I need a rest. Are you a customer or a visitor?'

'A visitor. I called by to see how you are.'

'Everyone's treating me with kid gloves, but I don't really need it. I'm fine.'

'That's good.'

'Tom has talked me out of feeling responsible for what happened to Mrs Dryden. He says it's nonsense to think like that.'

'He's quite right. You weren't responsible, Ruth. Not in any way.'

'Still, it was pretty awful, wasn't it?'

'Yes, it was. But you must put it out of your mind. You've got other things to think of.'

'That's just what Tom keeps telling me. She wasn't very well liked in the village, you know. Some people were actually rather glad to be rid of her. Flora Bentley said she upset the equilibrium of Frog End – whatever that's supposed to mean.'

He understood Mrs Bentley's sentiment well enough but it was hard to imagine the habitual poacher of fête trestle tables for her cake stall going so far as to steal the EpiPen. Or anyone else doing it, for that matter, unless Mrs Pudsey's long-simmering umbrage had finally boiled over? In any case, it was a subject best avoided with Ruth.

He said, 'Can I change to being a customer now?'

'Of course you can, Hugh. You're one of my best.'

'How would I go about growing bluebells?'

Like the Major, Freda Butler was trying to brace herself – not to enter into the Christmas spirit because she had never been able to do that, at least, not wholeheartedly. She could not remember how things had been when her mother was alive, but her father, the Admiral, had had more than a touch of Scrooge about him. In his view, Christmas trees were German and therefore forbidden, while turkeys, being American, were also banned. Carols, he had maintained, had mostly been composed by foreigners, and presents were a waste of money. It was all humbug to him.

While she had been serving in the WRNS, Christmas had been quite enjoyable. There was usually a station dance and a turkey lunch where officers traditionally served other ranks. She had always volunteered for extra duty, having no proper home to go to. On retirement, though, she had found herself faced with Christmases spent awkwardly with the long-retired Admiral and, after his death, alone. Last year, Mrs Latimer, who ran the bookstall at the summer fête, had been kind enough to invite her for lunch but the gathering had also included Mrs Latimer's son and daughter-in-law with three very noisy and badly behaved small children. She had been rather relieved to escape back to the peace and quiet of Lupin Cottage.

But something other than Christmas was bothering Miss Butler. Her mind kept going back to the evening at the Manor when Mrs Dryden had had the great misfortune to suffer a fatal allergic attack after eating one of the mince pies. It had been quite shocking. Not being a natural mingler at parties, Miss Butler tended to keep in the background and to observe. What she had observed had not struck her as at all significant at the time, but since reading Mrs Dryden's obituary in the newspaper and noticing an odd coincidence, she had been wondering whether or not she should speak to someone about it. There was only one person in the village whom she could trust implicitly. The Colonel. He would know the right thing to do.

She had been keeping Pond Cottage under close surveillance through the Zeiss binoculars while she was summoning up the nerve to walk across the village green and knock on the front door. She had also been inventing excuses for herself not to go. The Colonel would very likely be in his shed, busy with some kind of woodwork, in which case he would not hear her knock. It was out of the question to go round the back and knock on the shed door; unthinkable to disturb him. And if she did tell him about the odd coincidence, he would probably think she had gone completely batty.

She lifted the binoculars once again and trained them on the cottage, searching for signs of life. It was generally understood that the Colonel always took a sandwich to the shed with him for his lunch, but that he usually returned to the cottage later for a cup of tea. If she waited for, say, another half hour, she might catch him at just the right moment. It seemed important not to let much more time pass, not to delay doing what needed to be done. It was her duty, after all. But she needed a respectable reason for calling on a gentleman, especially after dark. If only she could think of one.

The Colonel had put the kettle on to boil when he heard the timid knock at the front door. After several hours spent working on the rocking horse's legs he was looking forward to a cup of tea and, later on, an even more restorative glass of whisky. Unfortunately, he had already switched on the sitting-room lamps and closed the curtains so whoever it was knocking would deduce that he was at home. In his experience, the inhabitants of Frog End were ruthlessly persistent when calling, so there was little point in pretending that he was out. He left the kettle to switch itself off and went to the door.

'I'm so sorry to trouble you, Colonel. Do forgive me.'

He was very surprised to see his visitor. She seldom called at the cottage and never after dark.

'That's quite all right, Miss Butler. Would you like to come in?'

'I'm sure you must be busy working.'

She would know all about the shed and probably the rocking horse, too. Perhaps she would even know that he had now cut out the four legs and finished sanding them, ready for the next stage? Information on his progress seemed to leak out of the shed and penetrate the village by some strange kind of osmosis.

'I've just knocked off for the day. Would you like a cup of tea?'

'Oh, no . . .'

'Well, at least come inside out of the cold.' He coaxed her over the threshold, down the hallway and into the sitting room. 'Do sit down. I'll light the fire.'

She perched timidly on the edge of the sofa, her navy blue handbag resting on her knees. He had never seen her dressed in anything but navy blue. Her years in the WRNS seemed to have dyed her indelibly in that colour. She was sitting well away from Thursday who, in any case, ignored her, feigning sleep, though he would certainly be perfectly aware that she was there. The clue was the occasional twitch of his tail. Miss Butler was not a cat person, nor a dog one either, so far as the Colonel was aware. Thursday would tolerate her presence so long as she kept her distance and made no false moves.

He struck a match and soon the log fire was burning brightly. 'Are you quite sure you won't have some tea?'

'No, really, Colonel. I mustn't stay long.'

'There's no rush, so far as I'm concerned.' He sat down in his wing chair and smiled at her encouragingly. 'I think it might be going to snow, don't you? We could be in for a White Christmas.'

'Yes, we could.'

'Will you be going away?'

'Oh, no. I never do now. After I retired from the WRNS I used to spend Christmas with my father but, of course, he passed away several years ago.'

The late and fearsome Admiral whose studio portrait in full dress uniform dominated Lupin Cottage looked unlikely to have been very merry company. Poor Miss Butler.

He said, 'We service people were lucky, weren't we? Christmas was always well celebrated. Very convivial.'

'Yes, indeed.'

Silence fell again. The Colonel took a stab in the dark. 'Did you want to ask me about something?'

Miss Butler fumbled nervously in her handbag and pulled out a folded news cutting.

'I was just wondering if you might like to contribute to this, Colonel? Knowing how kind you were in helping with the Save the Donkey collection.' She proffered the cutting. 'It's a very worthy cause.'

He took it and saw that the appeal was not for ill-treated donkeys this time but for dancing bears. The accompanying photo was of a female black bear with a rope tied through her pierced nose and who had, apparently, been made to dance on the streets of India for twelve years. She had been saved by an international animal rescue organization and now lived in a bear sanctuary. He had thought that making bears dance to entertain people belonged to a grim and distant past but, of course, in truth there was no end to the cruel treatment of animals.

'I'd be glad to make a donation.'

'That's so kind of you.'

He fetched his cheque book and unscrewed the cap of his fountain pen to write. 'I hope this will be of some help.'

'How very generous of you, Colonel. I will send it to the rescue organization. They will be so grateful.'

There was no way of knowing whether the appeal was genuine or whether any of the money given would actually be spent on wretched bears like the one in the photograph. All one could do was hope so.

Miss Butler had put his cheque away carefully in her navy

blue handbag and snapped the clasp shut, but she stayed where she was and he realized that the visit was not yet over. The bears had been an excuse, rather than the real reason. He waited patiently.

At last, she said, 'I've had something on my mind lately that's been troubling me, Colonel. I'm not quite sure what I should do about it.'

He seemed to have missed his vocation. He should have been a priest, not a soldier – hearing people's confidences and confessions, dispensing comfort and absolution. Given that he was a non-believer, it was rather ironic. Whatever Miss Butler's problem was, he hoped it was nothing spiritual.

'Perhaps I could help, if you'd like to tell me about it.'

'I notice things, you see. I'm very observant.'

He thought of the German U-boat commander's binoculars sweeping across Frog End village green as assiduously as they had done over the wastes of the North Atlantic.

'Yes, I'm sure you are.'

'I don't go out to social occasions very often. I'm afraid I've never been very good at them. I find them rather an ordeal.'

'They certainly can be.'

'But I was at the Manor on that unfortunate evening when Mrs Dryden was taken ill. I was standing by myself, watching the scene, as it were, and I happened to see her taking a mince pie from Mrs Jay. Mrs Peabody had tried to offer one of hers but Mrs Jay got there first. Elbowed her aside, actually. Quite rudely. Of course, I didn't think anything of it at the time. It was only later when I read about the cause of death in the newspaper that I realized the significance. They were very delicious-looking mince pies, you see. They had pastry stars on the top, sprinkled with icing sugar, like snow. I thought that if they came my way, I should like to try one.'

He remembered how good they had looked and tasted. 'Yes, they were excellent.'

'Mrs Jay was carrying them very nicely arranged on a glass cake dish – the old-fashioned kind with three tiers – and she held it up to Mrs Dryden by the handle at the top. Do you know what it reminded me of, Colonel?'

'I can't say that I do.'

'It made me think of *Snow White*.'

He failed to see why.

'Snow White?'

'The Walt Disney film. My mother took me to see it when I was seven years old and I can still vividly remember the scene where the evil queen comes to the cottage door disguised as an old peddler woman and offers Snow White a shiny poisoned apple. She offered it up in exactly the same way as Mrs Jay held up her mince pies to Mrs Dryden and with the same sort of look on her face. Enticing her. Of course, I had no idea then that they would be poisonous to Mrs Dryden.'

The film had obviously made a deep impression.

'None of us had, Miss Butler.'

'Oh, but you see, Colonel, I think Mrs Jay knew.'

He looked at her. So far as he knew, Miss Butler was not in the habit of making wild and unfounded accusations.

'Why would you think that?'

'Because it's such a strange coincidence.'

'What is, Miss Butler?'

She fiddled nervously with the clasp of her handbag, clicking it open and snapping it shut several times.

'I really oughtn't to say anything . . .'

'It might stop you worrying.'

She took a deep breath. 'Well, when Mrs Jay first moved into Frog End, I called on her. People don't bother to do that much nowadays, I'm afraid, but I felt obliged, knowing that she was on her own, like myself. She rents Farthings – it's the last house on the left going out on the road to Dorchester. Rather a shabby-looking place, really. The owners have gone off to New Zealand for five years or more. Such a long way away. Twelve thousand miles, I believe. I don't think I'd care to live there, would you, Colonel? Though I hear they're very nice people and quite similar to us, much more so than the Australians. Not that I've ever actually met an Australian, except one. He was a sub-lieutenant who was born in Perth but moved to England, so I never felt he really counted, though he did speak oddly.'

He steered her back to the point – whatever it was. 'What exactly was the coincidence that has been bothering you so much, Miss Butler?'

'A name.'

'A name?'

'A very unusual one. You see, Mrs Jay was kind enough to offer me a cup of tea and while I was sitting drinking it, I noticed a framed photograph of a young girl on the table beside me. When I remarked on it, Mrs Jay told me that it was her daughter, Xanthe. I'd never heard the name before and she said that it was the name of a sea nymph in Greek mythology who was one of the daughters of Oceanus. It means "Golden One". She spelled it out for me. X- A- N- T- H- E. You can say it in several different ways, apparently, but she pronounced it Zan-thay. It must be rather trying to have a name beginning with an "x" that's like a "z" and having to spell it for people all the time, don't you think? Like some of those peculiar Irish ones. Personally, I prefer simpler names, though those seem to have gone out of fashion. Children are called all sorts of things, like after London boroughs and days of the week. Anyway, I said how unusual it was and how charming the girl looked. And then Mrs Jay told me that she'd died years ago. Of course, I said how very sorry I was and how dreadful it must have been. It's always hard to find the right words, isn't it?'

'Very hard.'

'I'd forgotten all about the name until I read Mrs Dryden's obituary in the newspaper. It said about her once being a famous model and it mentioned that Mr Dryden had left his first wife for her. Xanthe Dryden committed suicide as a result, they said. It made me wonder if, by any chance, Mrs Jay's daughter and Mr Dryden's first wife could have been the same person.'

The Colonel was remembering his conversation with Kenneth Dryden. *I left my first wife for Joan, you know. Xanthe committed suicide. Hanged herself. It was ghastly.*

'I'm sure it's just a coincidence.'

'But it might not be. It is a very unusual name, isn't it?'

He said slowly, 'Yes, it is.'

'And Mrs Jay might have held a long-standing grudge against Mr and Mrs Dryden – especially against Mrs Dryden for stealing her daughter's husband and causing her to take her own life. That must have been so terrible. If Mrs Jay knew about the allergy it was a very clever way to take her revenge.'

The unremarkable and kindly cat lover he'd met seemed to have somehow metamorphosed into a vengeful hag offering deadly mince pies, while the previously evil Snow Queen had suddenly turned into innocent Snow White. First Kenneth Dryden and now Miss Butler had allowed their imaginations to run riot.

He said, 'Mrs Jay knew nothing about the allergy and she seemed very upset about what happened.'

'She could have been lying and it would be easy to pretend to be upset, wouldn't it? I remember that when Mrs Dryden was searching for her spectacles at the first read-through, she took a lot of things out of her handbag and put them on the table. I was watching her, you see, and I particularly noticed a strange tube-shaped object with blue and orange ends and wondered what it was. I'm quite sure now that it must have been the EpiPen that she was always supposed to carry with her. Other people would have seen it, including Mrs Jay, who was there too.'

He said soothingly, 'I don't think there's any need for you to upset yourself, Miss Butler. Nobody was to blame for Mrs Dryden's death. It was a sad accident. The post-mortem confirmed it.'

'I wish I could believe that, Colonel. But I simply can't get it out of my mind. I wonder, would you go and call on Mrs Jay and find out whether her daughter was Mr Dryden's first wife? If she wasn't, then of course there's nothing for me to worry about.'

'And if she was?'

'You'll know what to do.'

He escorted her home across the green, shining a torch for her. At the neat little white-painted gate of Lupin Cottage she thanked him several times.

'You've taken such a load off my mind, Colonel. I shall be able to sleep soundly tonight.'

He knew how Henry V must have felt on the night before the battle of Agincourt, wandering disguised among his soldiers. *Upon the king! Let us our lives, our souls, our debts, our careful wives, our children and our sins lay on the king! We must bear all.*

Miss Butler was counting on him to sort things out for her so that she could sleep at night.

Thursday had abandoned the sofa and was waiting in the kitchen for supper to be served. Miraculously, the Munchies Grilled Fish Medley, as recommended by nice Mrs Jay, still seemed to be in favour. After the routinely wary start, the Colonel left the old cat deigning to eat and went to pour himself an early whisky. He put another log on the fire and sat down.

Freda Butler's confidence was entirely misplaced. If Kenneth Dryden's abandoned first wife turned out to be Thora Jay's deceased daughter, he had no idea what should be done – if anything. It was no more proof of malicious intent on Mrs Jay's part than Kenneth's stubborn and baseless contention that Clarissa had deliberately taken the EpiPen from her mother's handbag.

He pictured himself solemnly reporting Miss Butler's Snow White fantasy to a police officer – say, Detective Inspector Squibb of the Dorset Police who had handled the investigation into Lady Swynford's murder at the Manor last year, as well as the supposed suicide of the actress, Lois Delaney. A sharply dressed young man, thin-lipped and with a sardonic attitude.

It was easy to imagine the inspector's response.

'We get a lot of that sort of thing from elderly ladies, Colonel. You'd be surprised at the tales they spin. They seem to like the attention.'

'Miss Butler is the kind of person who would go to great lengths to avoid attracting attention to herself. She was very reluctant to say anything to me but she seemed quite sure about what she saw.'

'I dare say, sir. But there's no need for her to concern herself. The deceased in question died from acute anaphylactic shock brought on by a severe allergy to almonds.' The inspector would smirk. 'Nobody gave her a poisoned apple.'

'Her EpiPen was missing from her handbag; otherwise she might have been saved.'

'People get careless, sir. They forget their pills and potions or take the wrong ones. It happens all the time.'

Tom Harvey had said much the same thing.

'The Pen is still missing.'

'I've no doubt it will turn up eventually. Things usually do. Now, if you'll excuse me, sir, I've got plenty of real work to do.'

The Colonel considered his glass for a moment. The poisoned apple had only sent Snow White into a deep sleep and a handsome prince had wakened her with a kiss. Joan Dryden had not been so fortunate.

After the dress rehearsal, he remembered her remarking that she and Thora Jay had got on surprisingly well. *I practically told her my life story*. The story could easily have included the fact that she was extremely allergic to nuts. Also, if Kenneth Dryden's first wife had been Mrs Jay's daughter, then she would have been bound to know a good deal about the woman who had stolen her daughter's husband and driven her to suicide. She would have read about her in newspapers and magazines, listened to gossip about her, probably heard about the emergency dashes to hospital. And, when it came to taking the EpiPen, it would have been a simple matter for her to do so while the bag was in the village hall dressing room and the Snow Queen safely occupied on stage. Or, perhaps, later at the Manor when it had been left unguarded on a chair, though that was less likely as well as more risky.

But, if Thora Jay had once been Kenneth Dryden's mother-in-law, why hadn't he noticed her at the Players' rehearsals or at the performances where he had been very much in attendance? Men usually remembered their mothers-in-law, even though they might sometimes prefer to forget them.

Certainly, Naomi's comment about Mrs Jay being unnoticeable had some truth in it. He himself had failed to place her when he had bumped into her in the pet shop in Dorchester. And it must be eighteen years or more since Kenneth had walked out on her daughter. Enough time for someone to have changed out of recognition, or simply faded from memory.

He had promised Miss Butler that he would find an excuse to call on Mrs Jay, but he was blessed if he could think of one. The poor wretched dancing bears wouldn't do, however worthy their cause. He'd have to think of something better than that.

He put on a favourite Gilbert and Sullivan record, hoping for inspiration to come to him as he listened.

'With cat-like tread,
Upon our prey we steal;
In silence dread,
Our cautious way we feel.
No sound at all!
We never speak a word;
A fly's footfall
Would be distinctly heard . . .'

As if on cue, Thursday made his entrance into the room, soundless and wordless. He sprang up on to the sofa and lay there, washing his whiskers with the satisfied air of one who has dined well. Thora Jay's recommendation in the pet shop had been a good one. The Colonel thought of their interesting cat chat. It would be perfectly understandable to consult her for more tips.

FIFTEEN

As Miss Butler had told him, Farthings was the last house on the road leading out of the village. The Colonel stopped the Riley outside the gate on his way to the pet shop in Dorchester. She had been right, too, about it being rather shabby. The front door and windows needed re-painting and the garden was sadly neglected – the fate of many a house with faraway owners. He rang the bell.

Thora Jay took some time to answer and, as he had expected, was startled to see him on her doorstep. He trotted out his lame excuse about needing another cat food recommendation.

'Of course, Colonel. I'll write down a few suggestions. Do come in.'

He stepped into the house, which was shabby inside as well as out, and followed her into a depressing kitchen obviously unchanged for decades. She opened a cupboard and took out several tins of Munchies cat food, aligning them on the table.

'All these have been tested by my cat and met with her full approval. And that's not easily given, I can tell you.'

He picked the tins up in turn and read their contents. Duck slowly cooked in a sauce with garden vegetables, Pacific tuna and whitebait caught fresh from the sea, using dolphin-friendly methods, chicken breasts with ham sauce, mouth-watering terrine of salmon.

'They sound good enough for human consumption.'

'Pet owners can be as particular as their pets. And cats are the most particular of all, as you and I know. I can give you a demonstration, if you like. Here is Mabel.'

He turned to see a cat sitting behind him. Like Thursday, her entry had been soundless.

'What a fine-looking animal.'

'She's a pedigree British Blue.'

He admired the dense blue coat and the copper eyes. 'I'm afraid my cat is just a stray old moggy.'

'They're sometimes the most interesting. I'll open a tin of the duck. It's one of her favourites.'

He watched the cat walk straight up to the bowl and crouch down to begin eating without any hesitation. No suspicious sniffing, no cautious circling, no ungrateful rejection. Miraculous.

'I'm very impressed.'

She handed him the list she had written. 'These are all good. I'm sure your cat will approve. Would you like a cup of tea before you go? I usually have one at about this time.'

He waited while she put the kettle on to boil, took down a teapot and set out cups and saucers on a tray.

'Have you lived in Frog End long, Mrs Jay?'

'Three years. I came here from London soon after I'd retired. I liked the idea of village life but it hasn't worked out quite the way I hoped.'

'What a pity.'

'The people are very friendly and I've enjoyed being a member of the Players and one or two of the clubs, but city life suits me better. As a matter of fact, I'm planning to move to Canada. I have some cousins in Vancouver and they have been urging me to go and live there with them.'

'I hear it's very beautiful.'

'So they keep telling me.'

'What about Mabel?'

'I'll take her with me. She's very adaptable and Canada doesn't quarantine domestic cats.'

She had set the tea things on a tray and he carried it through to the sitting room for her. She lit the gas fire. 'Sit down, Colonel.'

As he did so, he saw the framed photograph of a young girl on the table next to him. Miss Butler must have sat in exactly the same place.

He leaned a little closer to see it better. The girl had long dark hair and she was smiling.

'Sugar, Colonel?'

'No, thank you.'

He took the cup of tea that Thora Jay held out to him.

'That's my daughter you were looking at. It was taken when she was sixteen.'

'She's lovely.'

'Yes, she was. Luckily, she didn't take after me. She got her looks from her father. Unfortunately, he died soon after she was born.'

'I'm sorry to hear that.'

'Xanthe herself died when she was only twenty-two.'

'How very sad.'

She sat down opposite him, stirring her tea calmly. 'She was married to Kenneth Dryden before he left her for Joan Lowe. Normally, I never talk about it at all, Colonel, but I feel I can to you. In private.'

He should have known that Miss Butler would have guessed right about the name.

'Of course.'

'She was much younger than him, you see. He was already well-known for his television programmes. Rather a glamorous figure – much better looking than he is now. They met when she was working as an assistant on a television documentary he was making in Guatemala. I suppose it was inevitable that she would fall for him. They were married in Florida soon afterwards but I didn't meet Kenneth until they eventually came back to England. Xanthe was obviously deeply in love and he seemed very happy with her. She went on several of his trips and had a wonderful time. Life was idyllic for two years, until he met Joan Lowe. Joan took him away from Xanthe, Colonel. And she had no compunction in doing so. No conscience whatever. Some women are like that, aren't they?'

'Kenneth Dryden must have had some choice in the matter.'

'He's a weak man, for all his success. Haven't you noticed?'

'I don't know him well enough to say.'

'But I'm sure you're a very good judge of character. He walked out on Xanthe without hesitation and left her completely devastated – in a most terrible mental and physical state. She came to live with me in my flat in London and seemed to be getting better, but then, one day I came home from work and found her dead in her room. She'd hanged herself, Colonel. Made a noose for her neck with a belt tied round a heavy curtain rod, stood on a chair and kicked it over. She left me a note saying that she didn't want to live any more.'

He said quietly, 'It must have been dreadful for you.'

'It was. I got on with my life, but I had lost my only child, as well as my husband, so there didn't seem much point to it any more. I still had my work, of course, but once I'd retired that was gone too. I had moved to Frog End, joined the Players and was beginning to find my feet when the Drydens bought Hassels. You can imagine how I felt about that, especially when Joan was given the part of the Snow Queen.'

'I'm surprised that Kenneth Dryden didn't recognize you at the rehearsals.'

'I'm not a very memorable person, Colonel. It can sometimes be an advantage. He and I only met once or twice. He was often away, and a very busy man. Being nice to mothers-in-law wasn't really his style. And I had never met Joan before.'

'You can't have enjoyed doing her make-up.'

'I've always taken a strictly professional view of my work, Colonel. It's immaterial to me whether I like the person or not.'

He drank some tea. 'I wonder; did she ever talk to you about her allergy to nuts?'

'No. We talked about make-up and modelling and actor gossip. And about how impossible her daughter was. Of course, I could have mentioned that my own daughter was dead because of her, but I didn't.'

'Mrs Dryden was supposed to carry an EpiPen in her bag to use if she had an anaphylactic attack. Did you happen to notice if she had it with her at the village hall that evening?'

'No, I didn't, Colonel. I don't know what an EpiPen looks like. I've never even seen one. It wasn't in her bag when she had the attack at the Manor, was it? So I imagine she must have left it at home. Very careless of her. And she paid the price.'

'A very high one. Doesn't that worry you?'

'Worry me? You mean because it was one of my mince pies that poisoned her? No, not at all. I'm not sorry she's dead, Colonel, and I won't pretend to you that I am because that would be hypocritical. On the contrary, I'm glad. And I'm sure I'm not the only one. People like her always think they can get away with everything in life but, in the end, of course, they can't.'

He put down his cup. 'Well, I won't keep you any longer, Mrs Jay.'

'You've forgotten your list, Colonel.'

'I must have left it in the kitchen.'

She fetched it and he put it away in his pocket.

She said, 'I hope your cat likes them.'

'So do I.'

At the front door she looked up at him with her blank and unmemorable face. But he saw the look of triumph in her eyes.

'So far as I'm concerned, Colonel, justice has been done. That's all I have to say. And all I'll ever say.'

As he drove on to Dorchester, the spectre of Detective Inspector Squibb reappeared before him.

'So, you think that Mrs Jay knew all about Mrs Dryden's nut allergy?'

'I think Mrs Dryden talked to her about it when she was having her Snow Queen make-up done for the dress rehearsal. Or that she'd already learned about it beforehand. According to Miss Butler, Mrs Jay could easily have seen the EpiPen when Joan Dryden emptied out her handbag at the play read-through, looking for her spectacles. In which case, she would have known then, if not before, that Joan Dryden had some kind of serious allergy. Not too difficult to find out exactly what it was when she was talking to her later at the dress rehearsal.'

'Why would Mrs Jay lie to you?'

'To admit that she knew about the nut allergy would have meant that she must have offered up the almond mince pies deliberately to Mrs Dryden, knowing they would poison her, instead of warning her against them. And it would have been easy for her to remove the EpiPen from Mrs Dryden's bag in the village hall dressing room when she was on stage. The Pen had to be taken before the Manor party for Mrs Jay's plan to succeed, Inspector. She had to persuade Mrs Dryden to take one of her mince pies before she had the chance to take a harmless one from somebody else. At the Manor Christmas party, guests traditionally only have one mince pie. More might not leave enough to go round. Mrs Jay's lucky break was that the host, Doctor Harvey, had been called out to a patient, otherwise he could have treated Mrs Dryden.'

The inspector was wearing his most sardonic expression.

'You seem to have it all worked out, Colonel. And what was Mrs Jay's motive, may I ask?'

'Revenge. Her daughter, Xanthe, was the first wife of Mr Dryden. After he left her for Joan Lowe she committed suicide. She hanged herself.'

'And when did that happen?'

'About eighteen years ago.'

'That's a very long wait for vengeance.'

'It's said to be a dish better served cold, isn't it, Inspector? Time and chance eventually provided Thora Jay with the perfect opportunity. She could give her victim what she knew would be poison to her but innocuous to others, and, at the same time, take away the means of her survival.'

'So far, you haven't provided a shred of evidence for me, sir. I can't make an arrest just because some batty old maid like your Miss Butler imagined they saw a funny look on somebody's face when they were handing round their mince pies. You'll have to do much better than that.'

'Mrs Jay was responsible for Joan Dryden's death, Inspector. I'm sure of it. Isn't malice aforethought a definition of murder? She had plenty of malice and plenty of time to think about it.'

'Show me an iota of proof, Colonel. Proof that Mrs Jay knew about Mrs Dryden's allergy and took away her EpiPen with harmful intent.'

'I'm afraid I don't have any proof.'

'Then there's nothing I can do. You'll pardon me for saying it, sir, but you amateur sleuths are no help to us in the police force. We haven't got time to go off on wild goose chases where there's no case. Let's just forget all about it, shall we?'

The Colonel called at Lupin Cottage on his way back from Dorchester, tins of Munchies rattling on the passenger seat beside him. Miss Butler opened the door and led him into her pin-neat little sitting room. His arrival must have taken her by surprise because she had left the U-boat commander's binoculars on the table by the window. They were usually kept out of sight.

'Did you go to see Mrs Jay, Colonel?'

'Yes, I did. You were quite right, Miss Butler. Mrs Jay's daughter was Mr Dryden's first wife.'

She sank down on to a chair, hand to her mouth. 'Oh dear, oh dear. I was afraid of that.'

He said calmly, 'There's nothing to be afraid of. Mrs Jay assured me that she had no idea that Mrs Dryden was allergic to nuts.'

'But I saw the look on her face, Colonel. Just like in Snow White. She was willing Mrs Dryden to take one.'

'Well, they did look very good, didn't they? And I'm sure she was proud of them and wanted them to be appreciated. They were certainly much more appealing than Mrs Peabody's.'

Miss Butler nodded. 'That's very true.'

'As it happened, of course, Mrs Peabody's would have been far better for Mrs Dryden.'

Miss Butler shook her head. 'No, they wouldn't, Colonel. Mrs Peabody always makes her mince pies with lots of almonds. She told me so. It's an old recipe of her mother's.'

Life had its unexpected ironies, the Colonel thought. Thora Jay needn't have gone to all the trouble of making her delicious-looking sugar-dusted pastry stars and elbowing old Mrs Peabody aside. Simply removing the EpiPen would have done the trick. Though whether Joan would ever have taken one of Mrs Peabody's disasters was questionable.

Fate, it seemed, had loaded the dice unfairly against Joan. Nuts aplenty. No EpiPen. No Tom Harvey close at hand to save her.

'Well, there's nothing more for you to do, Miss Butler, and nothing more for you to worry about.'

She gave a deep sigh of relief. 'Thank you, Colonel. You're always such a comfort.'

Thursday wandered into the kitchen and took up his position in front of his bowl. The time had come to put a tin of Munchies to the test.

The Colonel took a moment to choose and, in the end, went

for the Tempting Terrine of Salmon. He scooped a small
amount into the bowl and stood back. As usual, Thursday took
his time, sniffing suspiciously at it. The Colonel held his breath
and his spoon, not daring to move. A cautious step forward
and more sniffing. Another step. And another. More sniffing.
A tentative nibble. And, wonder of wonders, Thursday crouched
down and started to eat.

Whether Thora Jay had been lying or not, when it came to
brands of cat food she had been telling him nothing but the
truth.

SIXTEEN

'I've made up my mind, Roger. I'm resigning.'

The Major lowered his newspaper warily. The old girl had plonked herself down on the sofa opposite him, feet planted wide apart, legs more than ever like the Shangri-La gateposts. Not a good sign.

'From what, exactly?'

She had fingers in many pies, and it could be any one of them.

'The Frog End Players, of course. I've decided it's time to hand over the reins. I'm simply wasting my time trying to raise standards, to produce something of real quality. The village is only interested in vulgar pantomimes and Agatha Christie murders.'

He didn't argue the point, mainly because it was true, but also because he'd be treading on thin ice. Marjorie had by no means forgotten the polar bear.

'If that's what you've decided.'

'Everyone seemed to have found Mr Jugge's antics highly amusing but, of course, he completely ruined the play.'

'I wouldn't say that.'

'No, you wouldn't, Roger. But I do. All that hard work of mine and I might just as well not have bothered. Well, someone else can take on the job next time. I'm having nothing more to do with the Players.'

'In that case, I'll resign too. Keep a united front.'

She said caustically, 'I doubt if that will be much of a sacrifice for you.'

In his heart, the Major was rejoicing, though he was very careful not to show it. No more heaving scenery around! No more dogsbody fetching and carrying! No more interminable hours of dreary boredom! Praise be to Allah!

To his relief, Marjorie didn't stay long. Her ladies' bridge four called and, as soon as he heard the front door slam, the Escort stutter into life and the clashing of gears as she backed it out on to the road, he put aside his newspaper and headed straight for the cocktail cabinet.

There was no need for stealth or subterfuge. She would be away for three hours or more. He let 'Drink to Me Only With Thine Eyes' peal out merrily as he poured himself a nice little snifter. Back in his armchair he raised his glass to a golden future without the Frog End Players.

Rum business, though, about Joan Dryden. Here one day, gone the next. Not everyone's cup of tea, it must be said. She'd struck him as a pretty tough nut but she'd made a damned good Snow Queen, there was no denying it. Rotten luck about taking the wrong mince pie and not having that thingamajig at the ready in her handbag, though.

Still, if it was true about the husband selling Hassels, it would mean other people moving in. New blood. Not a bad thing for Frog End, when he thought about it. The Drydens would never have fitted in, long term. Not really the type at all.

The pre-Christmas garden talk at the Manor was entitled No Plant is An Island. An intriguing slant on John Donne's perception, the Colonel thought, and decided to attend. Ruth chose her speakers well and, like Naomi, this one would certainly know what he was talking about.

There was a capacity audience of keen gardeners crammed into the Manor's panelled drawing room – scene of the summer fête committee meetings that the Colonel had attended as treasurer.

This time, instead of arguments over trestle tables, teacups and entrance prices, he listened with interest to the expert explaining that every plant grown interacts with the companion plants around it. It could dominate or it could be kept in check by them. Plants could offer benefits to their neighbours – support, shade, attract beneficial insects, distract potential pests. Therefore, it made good sense to avoid planting large blocks of the same plant but to mix them up rather like guests at a successful party. It was also a good idea to grow plenty of flowers in order to draw in pollinators, as well as scented herbs to confuse pests guided by scent.

The Colonel was gratified to learn that he had planted the right sort of things – rosemary, primroses, lavender, thyme, foxglove, echinops, sedum, aconites, his favourite hellebores, all apparently working their magic at different times of the year.

The speaker also had useful tips for encouraging wildlife into the garden. A population of predators would help keep pests in check, he said. Slug-devouring frogs and hedgehogs, aphid-hoovering hoverflies, pollinating bees and even wasps were the gardener's friend, he assured his attentive audience. A log pile left to rot and collapse made a perfect haunt for beetles and spiders and other helpful allies. Homes could be created for solitary bees by drilling holes in a block of wood placed somewhere sheltered, and a stack of bricks constructed with wide gaps left between them, stuffed with straw, twigs or perennial plant stems would create a Travelodge wildlife hotel to suit different creatures.

The Colonel could see Naomi sitting on the other side of the room, wearing one of her more muted tracksuits. She would approve no end, he knew. She had always preached against too much tidying up and sweeping.

'Leave the bloody leaves and stuff,' she'd told him. 'They'll give shelter to some useful creepy-crawlies and things you'll want on your side.'

He also noticed Thora Jay among the listeners, which surprised him. The garden at Farthings where she had lived for three years had looked totally neglected. There had been no sign that she had taken any interest in it, and had no need to have one now since she would soon be moving away to Canada.

Later that evening, Ruth phoned him. 'Jacob has found the EpiPen, Hugh. He's been sweeping the drive verges and, apparently, it was under some dead leaves. He brought it to show me. Of course, he had no idea what it was.'

The gardener employed at the Manor was a very shy, inarticulate man. A bit odd, it had to be said, and painfully clumsy in his movements, except where his work was concerned. Nobody knew much about his past. He had turned up at the Manor one day, out of the blue. Rather like Thursday, the

Colonel had sometimes thought, except that Thursday was a very different character.

It had been Jacob who had hacked down the impenetrable jungle of brambles and nettles at Pond Cottage, under Naomi's direction, and Jacob who had later laid the old stone slabs to make the sundowner terrace at the back, so persistently recommended by Naomi. Lady Swynford had sacked the poor man just before her death, but Ruth had kept him on and he had repaid her with devotion.

Ruth went on: 'It must have fallen out of her bag when the Drydens arrived for the party that evening.'

He said, 'Yes, it looks like that must have happened.'

But he well remembered Kenneth Dryden wrenching open the neck of the bag and shaking it hard to disgorge the contents.

'I gave it to Tom. He felt it was probably better not to tell Mr Dryden because it could upset him, but I think he should know about it, don't you?'

'Yes,' he said. 'I do. Would you like me to tell him? I have his phone number and he asked me to call him if it was ever found.'

'That would be very kind, Hugh.'

The Colonel rang Kenneth Dryden immediately. 'I thought you'd like to know that the EpiPen has been found.'

'Where in God's name was it?'

'At the edge of the Manor drive. The gardener saw it when he was sweeping.'

'But I searched all the way down the drive.'

'It was hidden among some leaves.'

There was a pause at the other end. 'It must have fallen out of her bag when she got out of the car.'

'It would seem so.'

Another pause.

'Which means that Clarissa couldn't possibly have taken it before.'

'No, she couldn't.'

'I'm glad of that, Hugh. I got to thinking about everything, once I'd cooled down. The kid's had a pretty tough time, after all. Joan wasn't exactly the ideal mother, and I can't say I've been a much better father. We had a long talk and she broke down in tears – swore to heaven that she'd never touched the EpiPen.'

'I'm sure she was speaking the truth.'

'She must have been. I feel rather bad about things. I'll try to persuade her to stay on at the flat for the moment. See how it goes.'

'I think it will work out all right.'

'Let's hope so, Hugh. I've already got a buyer for Hassels, so I doubt we'll meet again. I could send you tickets for one of my afternoon shows, if you like. We always have a live audience, though some of them seem brain-dead.'

'That's kind of you, but I'm not very often in London.'

'Well, you won't be missing much, to be honest.'

Another pause. 'Well, thank you for letting me know, Hugh. I appreciate it. Good luck with the rocking horse.'

'I'll need it.'

With Christmas only three days away, the Colonel had completed his preparations. Presents had been bought and wrapped for Susan, Marcus, Eric and Edith. Wine, chocolates and a colourful potted plant had been assembled. He had also added a bottle of Chivas Regal. Susan would probably disapprove but he was fairly sure that Marcus wouldn't. It was a pity that the rocking horse would have to wait for another time, but perhaps it was all for the best, considering that his granddaughter was still only six months old. Plenty of time to make a really good job of it. Perhaps even an heirloom.

He had packed a small case for himself – travelling light was something he had learned long ago – and Thursday had been booked into Cat Heaven for four days, though, fortunately, he didn't yet know it.

He was aware that the cottage looked sadly un-Christmassy. Kind people had sent cards, which he had put around, but he hadn't bothered with a tree this year. There had seemed no point since he'd be away. The box of decorations that Laura had collected and used over the years lay undisturbed up in the attic.

When the phone rang, he rather expected it to be Susan with final instructions. Instead, it was Alison, calling from the airport.

'I wanted to wish you a Happy Christmas, Dad.'

'Thank you. Happy Christmas to you, too. Have a wonderful time.'

'Don't let Susan sell you a bungalow.'

'Don't worry, I won't.'

Half an hour later, the phone rang and this time it was Susan, sounding very upset. 'Eric's gone down with chickenpox, Father.'

'Poor chap. I'm very sorry to hear that.'

'He's got spots all over him. The doctor says Edith will almost certainly catch it.'

'I wouldn't worry too much, Susan. At that age, it should be quite mild and it's probably good to get it over with.'

'Of course, we'll have to put you off, Father.'

'I had it years ago,' he said. 'I can't catch it again.'

'Oh, but I don't think we could cope, you see. Eric's running a high temperature and Edith is very fretful so I'm sure she's getting it. I'm very sorry, Father, but we won't be able to have you, after all. We'll have to cancel Christmas.'

He thought of his suitcase packed, the presents wrapped and ready, the potted plant, the chocolates, the wine and the bottle of Chivas Regal waiting obediently by the front door.

'I understand completely, Susan. I'll come and visit you another time. As soon as the children are better.'

'But will you be all right, Father? All on your own?'

'I won't be on my own,' he said. 'I'll have Thursday.'

He made the necessary call to Mrs Moffat at Cat Heaven. Thursday, snugly curled up at the fire end of the sofa, had no idea of his last-minute reprieve.

Naomi arrived as the grandfather clock was striking six. He unwound her from a moth-eaten fur wrap which shed brown tufts over the hall carpet.

'Another attic find?'

'Came across it when I was putting the polar bear back. I'd forgotten all about it. It belonged to a favourite great aunt. A Russian count who was her lover gave it to her. Sable, you know. Rather past its best now, but still useful if we get a cold snap.'

He followed her into the sitting room where the log fire was blazing, the Chivas Regal waiting, and Thursday, a tight black-and-tan ball, fast asleep on the sofa. Naomi moved him in one swift, smooth sideways movement, like a faultless rugger pass, and took his place. She was wearing a Father Christmas red tracksuit with her white moon-boot trainers.

The Colonel poured their first halves – her three fingers with a splash of water and no ice, his own without either. He raised his glass to her. 'Your Three Ships are out in time for Christmas, Naomi, just like you promised.' He had noticed the snowdrops that morning, ringing the lilac tree where he had planted them.

'Jolly good.'

'And Ruth's hellebores are flowering away. I don't know how they manage it in this weather.'

'They're much tougher than they look. Don't forget I'll let you have some of my December Dawn in the spring.'

'I'll look forward to them. Ruth's promised me some bluebells. Proper English ones. I thought they'd look good in the long grass at the end of the garden.'

'They'd look wonderful.'

They talked garden talk for a while until Naomi changed the subject.

'I ran into Thora Jay in Dorchester today. She told me she's moving to Canada. But, of course, you already know.'

'What makes you think I do?'

'Your car was spotted outside Farthings the other day.'

'The Frog End KGB at work?'

'No. Flora Bentley passing on the way to Dorchester to take back her library books.'

'As it happened, Mrs Jay did mention it. I gather she has cousins in Vancouver.'

'Did she also happen to mention that her daughter was Kenneth Dryden's first wife and that she hanged herself when he dumped her for Joan?'

'Where did you hear that?'

'Oh, from somebody.'

Naomi was often discreet about her sources. It was one of the many things he liked about her.

'I've heard something else rather interesting too, Hugh.'

'Oh?'

'Joan's missing EpiPen has turned up. Apparently Jacob found it at the side of the Manor drive and handed it over to Ruth.'

'Yes, I knew about that.'

'You're a dark horse, sometimes, Hugh. Who told you?'

'Ruth. She phoned after that talk at the Manor. And I rang Kenneth Dryden to tell him. He'd asked me to let him know if it was ever found.'

'Perhaps it fell out of her bag when she was getting out of their car?'

'It certainly looks like it.'

'But I thought he'd hunted everywhere for it – searched high and low.'

'Apparently, it was hidden under some dead leaves.'

'All rather fishy, don't you think, Hugh?'

'What is?'

'That Joan Dryden ate an almond-loaded mince pie at the Manor bash and that the EpiPen which would have saved her life had fallen out of her handbag. I've been thinking some more along those lines.'

'What have you been thinking?'

'That it would be an absolutely foolproof way to bump someone off without getting caught. What a wheeze! The perfect crime! I thought Monica Pudsey might have had something to do with it except that her mince pies are uneatable, so it would never have worked. But Thora's were a work of art. Do you know what I reckon, Hugh?'

'No.'

'I reckon that Thora knew about Joan's nut allergy and grabbed her opportunity to take revenge on what had happened to her daughter. It wasn't chance at all; Thora planned it from start to finish.'

'You've been thinking far too much, Naomi.'

'So have you, Sherlock. And you've been thinking exactly the same as me, though you won't admit it. I think Thora pinched the EpiPen in the village hall dressing room sometime during the final performance, saw to it that Joan took one of her scrumptious mince pies at the party afterwards and waited for the worst to happen. The extra luck was that Tom had been called out.'

'That's all supposition.'

'Not quite. Why did Thora go to that No Plant is An Island talk at the Manor? She's never been to any of the talks before and the garden at Farthings is a mess. Answer me that.'

'I've no idea.'

'You know very well why, Hugh. It was so that she could dump the EpiPen by the drive and make it look as though it had fallen out of Joan's bag when she arrived for the party. So she could never be suspected of having anything to do with it.'

'She isn't.'

'She is by us. What are we going to do about it, Hugh?'

'Nothing,' he said, wondering how many more times he would be repeating the same mantra. 'Thora Jay told me she didn't know about the nut allergy and had never even seen an EpiPen.'

'Well, she would say that, wouldn't she?'

'There's no evidence, Naomi. She could easily have been telling the truth.'

'But she wasn't, was she? You and I know that.'

'Do we?'

'Yes, we do. You ought to tell that Inspector Squabb man about it, Hugh. The one who investigated Ursula Swynford's murder.'

'Squibb.'

'Whatever he's called. He's a nasty piece of work but at least he's a policeman. He could do something. Arrest Thora, for a start.'

'On what grounds? Being fishy isn't enough. There is no evidence at all that she knew anything about Joan's allergy or that she ever touched the EpiPen. None whatsoever. The police wouldn't waste their time on it. Fortunately, the law in England still requires conclusive proof before a person can be convicted of murder.

Naomi sighed. 'I suppose I got carried away.'

But in exactly the right direction, he thought. After eighteen years Thora Jay had taken her revenge. He had no doubts about it. In her view, justice had been done. In his, she had got away with murder.

He stood up. 'How about the other half?'

'I don't mind if I do.'

He refilled her glass and his own and returned to his wing chair. 'To your good health, Naomi.'

'And to yours, Hugh. Are you all ready for your trip up to Norfolk?'

'Plans have changed, as a matter of fact. My grandson has gone down with chicken pox. Christmas has been cancelled.'

'Sorry to hear that, Hugh. You're welcome to come and spend it with me instead, if you like.'

'That's kind of you, Naomi, but I'll be fine. Thursday and I will be festive together.'

'You'd be doing me a favour. Someone gave me a brace of pheasants and they've been hanging for four days. If I don't do something with them soon they'll fall down. Do you like pheasant?'

'Very much.'

'That's settled, then. I'll cook the damned things and you come over and help me eat them. You can bring the wine.'

'With pleasure.'

'I'll keep the giblets for Thursday, so he won't feel left out.'

Thursday, feigning dignified slumber, twitched one ear.

'He'll appreciate it.'

'I doubt it.'

She raised her glass to him once more. 'To our Christmas, then, Hugh. Let's make it a jolly, jolly one.'

'I'll drink to that, Naomi.'

He smiled at her. He knew exactly what he would take her as a present.